The Garden

This Large Print Book carries the
Seal of Approval of N.A.V.H.

The Garden

Mandy Belle

Thorndike Press • Waterville, Maine

Copyright © 2004 by Mandy Belle

Published in 2005 by arrangement with Belle Publishing.

Thorndike Press® Large Print Romance.

The tree indicium is a trademark of Thorndike Press.

The text of this Large Print edition is unabridged.
Other aspects of the book may vary from the original edition.

Set in 16 pt. Plantin by Christina S. Huff.

Printed in the United States on permanent paper.

Library of Congress Cataloging-in-Publication Data

Belle, Mandy, 1981–
    The garden / by Mandy Belle.
        p. cm.
    ISBN 0-7862-7429-8 (lg. print : hc : alk. paper)
    1. Family-owned business enterprises — Fiction.
    2. Inheritance and succession — Fiction.   3. Large type
    books.   I. Title.
    PR9199.4.B454G37 2005
    822′.92—dc22   2004029243

For heroes big and small
For my devoted family and friends
And for Chuck
Always, my dear, sweet Chuck

As the Founder/CEO of NAVH, the only national health agency solely devoted to those who, although not totally blind, have an eye disease which could lead to serious visual impairment, I am pleased to recognize Thorndike Press★ as one of the leading publishers in the large print field.

Founded in 1954 in San Francisco to prepare large print textbooks for partially seeing children, NAVH became the pioneer and standard setting agency in the preparation of large type.

Today, those publishers who meet our standards carry the prestigious "Seal of Approval" indicating high quality large print. We are delighted that Thorndike Press is one of the publishers whose titles meet these standards. We are also pleased to recognize the significant contribution Thorndike Press is making in this important and growing field.

Lorraine H. Marchi, L.H.D.
Founder/CEO
NAVH

★ Thorndike Press encompasses the following imprints: Thorndike, Wheeler, Walker and Large Print Press.

To be surrounded by beautiful things has much influence upon the human creature; to make beautiful things has more

— Charlotte Perkins Gilman

Chapter One

There was a joyful hum among the staff of the Carlton Mansion as preparations for the grandest night of the year began. The silver and gold decorations danced triumphantly throughout the grand foyer and hall, shimmering elegantly under the luster of soft chandelier and candle light. From the hand-embroidered detailing on the tablecloths to the endless rows of fitted chair slipcovers, everything blended perfectly to share in the splendor of the celebration. And this brilliant detail extended on and on throughout the foyer, the ballroom and the beautifully dressed terrace and gardens.

Imported Persian rugs warmed the caramel hardwood floors and the freshly polished crystal winked at the licking flames of the roaring fire. The household's finest silver gleamed with perfection, reflecting the busy scene.

The head keeper, Elizabeth, smiled to herself as she pressed each napkin with care into an elegant fold and adorned it with a gold ring beside each elaborate place setting. Fine German tapestries decorated the deep mahogany walls and the French doors teased as they offered a breathtaking view of the gardens beyond.

And they were breathtaking . . .

The terrace glittered as the garden staff hustled to hang the endless string of tiny white lights. Each light sparkled like a bright star against the black night, outlining every shrub, tree and moss-covered pathway. This breathtaking view extending outward for acres until it soon became impossible to distinguish ground from starlit sky.

This, it is said, is where the romance of the Carlton Mansion begins. On this magnificent terrace and at this precise view, the enchantment of the garden was known to be strongest.

The exquisite decorations went up with ease, as though the ancient walls of the mansion longed to be dressed for the occasion. And though the staff was terribly busy, even they could not stop themselves from interrupting their work for a stolen look at the awesome transformation taking place around them.

The preparations marked the arrival of a special day in the household. Julian Carlton's only daughter, Madison, was to celebrate her twenty-first birthday. A ball had been anticipated by all for years and now the special day had quickly arrived. It promised to be the grandest party the Carltons had ever thrown and they had thrown many a grand celebration. Yet this one in particular left staff, family and friends anxious to experience the festivities that awaited them. There was no doubt that the public's eyes would be scanning the newspaper and magazine racks the following morning for a glimpse into the Carlton world and the kind of celebration that only existed in the wildest of fantasies.

The Carlton family was not only known and loved by the elite group of family and friends they socialized with but were quite famous in other circles as well. Julian's grandfather, Bradley Carlton, had been one of the first wealthy men to settle in Southampton after making a large fortune in railroads in the early nineteen hundreds. And his first son, Blake, had been taught how to use that first stroke of luck to increase the family fortune through sound investments in the financial markets.

The family never suffered from the market's great fall or the many dips and pinnacles it rode over the decades. Their money had been invested so diversely and smartly that their fortune only flourished over the years. What had begun as a modest fortune quickly grew to astronomical wealth for the family and when Julian was born the first son of Blake, he too was taught the art of cultivating their old money. And, as hoped, Julian instantly took a great interest in expanding their many assets when he was introduced to the family business at eighteen. He went straight to work, after graduation, dominating Wall Street as one of the world's biggest investors and smartest business tycoons. Julian bought companies like candy yet studied the newspapers and financial reports like a priest would his Bible; with patient reverence. And he was certainly known worldwide for being the son of one of the oldest and richest families in America.

A century before, Bradley Carlton had earned both money and respect and though he enjoyed the ease his life allowed him, he was determined to keep the name Carlton a known and prosperous one. And so tradition became the new social norm for anyone inheriting the family fortune and name or marrying into it.

Bradley Carlton had imposed strict rules and standards on his wife and children. Decades later, Julian insisted on honoring the memory of his ancestors with the very traditions his father and grandfather had practiced and swiftly ingrained in him.

And Madison was the perfect heir to it all, although being the first and only daughter of the Carlton name and fortune wasn't always a desirable position to be placed in. Julian would have much preferred to stick to the tradition and have a male successor. But times were different, it was the twenty-first century after all and Julian and his wife, Victoria, had no other choice than to groom their little girl for the monumental task of heading the powerful household someday, with certain concession, of course.

In less than twenty-four hours, the newest heir to the Carlton fortune would finally be an adult and life in the mansion would never be the same again. In less than twenty-four hours, Madison Carlton would be celebrated by everyone who knew and loved her: friends, family and the envious world!

Chapter Two

Early morning rays bathed the Carlton Mansion, reaching out across the vast lands they owned and streaming steadily into the large windows. The sky was a stunning canvas as streaks of pastel watercolor spread with the rising of the sun. The sun shone bright and strong that morning and its heat went right to work warming the last of the lingering cool night air.

A growing ray fell across Elizabeth's eyes as she worked at the marble baking counter of the enormous kitchen. She quickly brushed a fallen strand of shimmering gray hair from her forehead with the back of her thick wrist and peered up through the cracked shutters at the new day's sky. She pushed the panes further open, letting the sun fill the enormous room, giving its dark marble counters and floors a majestic golden hue.

"Ah, what a beautiful day it will be," she said to herself, "just wonderful for Madison's special day."

"Joseph!" Elizabeth called out to her husband through the open window.

"Yes, Elizabeth, what is it? Is everything okay in there?" His answer came from the small electrical room below the kitchen's window. He was busy installing the timer on the garden lights for the party.

"Did you see that sunrise? What a sight! I shall remember that royal blue for when my brush meets palette next," Elizabeth called out through the enormous window as she kneaded dough for the evening's bread.

"You capturing that sight would be a sin, Elizabeth. It's the very reason I get out of bed so early every morning. You steal that sunrise and I'm likely to sleep past noon," he teased, double-checking he hadn't forgotten to disconnect the intricate sprinkler system.

Everything would be just right for this celebration, Joseph thought, not a thing could go wrong on such a wonderful occasion. He triple-checked just the same.

"Ah, a good mood my husband is in. What may have caused such a thing?" Elizabeth teased back and set the dough aside to rise.

Joseph locked the electrical room and came around to the kitchen's side entrance. Leaving his boots on the steps and entering with a look of mischief in his eye, he approached his wife.

"Just happy for Madison, sweet darling, that's all," he answered with a peck to her flour-dusted cheek.

"Ah, and so am I. Look how the bread is rising already, Joseph. It is a magical day," she exclaimed and clapped her hands in delight.

"Yes, magical. Were there problems in the dining hall last night?"

"No, why do you ask? Have you heard of problems?" Elizabeth held her breath.

"No, no, you were so late to rest. Where were you?"

"Ah, it was Madison. You know she has her father's nerves, the poor girl. She was up 'till midnight pacing that room of hers. It's all this fuss over her birthday, too much pressure on the thing." Elizabeth eased up onto her working stool and began mixing the filling for the desserts.

She was feeling the pressure herself yet she was enjoying the preparations for this party more than any other. This time it was all for Madison.

Elizabeth had a staff of four to help her with the desserts and a hired caterer would be arriving shortly to handle the extensive menu but she still insisted on getting her own arms elbow-deep in flour and sugar and doing as much as she could by her own hand.

And despite all the excitement, her heart ached as she thought of Madison. The poor girl was all wound up over the party and rightfully so. A celebration at the Carlton Mansion was never just that. Victoria and Julian outdid themselves every year and this year would be no different. Elizabeth looked out through the window. The sun was now climbing over the treetops and she remembered the night before.

Madison had lain sprawled across her bed. As Elizabeth stroked her golden hair, her head had rested lightly in her best friend's lap. The excitement had finally gotten to them both, Elizabeth exhausted from the day's work and Madison anxious about the party. So anxious, in fact, she couldn't even sleep.

They often stayed up late together when Madison let her nerves get the better of her. Elizabeth didn't mind; it was the only private time they got together now that she had grown out of pigtails. Elizabeth's life was to serve the Carlton household as well as oversee all other staff members. It was a lot of work for one woman yet quite an honor and she accepted it proudly.

She had lived and served in the Carlton

Mansion for almost fifty years. They were her family; it was her home. Though it left little time for herself or for Madison, Elizabeth loved her work for the Carltons and she adored the old mansion, especially the gardens and orchards. She always got a sense of serenity and regality from her walks through them. "It's a healing experience," she had often said.

Elizabeth was thoroughly convinced that the extensive grounds were what were keeping Julian with them long after the frightening diagnosis they had received two years ago. Through the worst of his condition, an afternoon among the flowers and trees could get him feeling better and back to his work within hours.

It was all truly remarkable and Elizabeth felt blessed to be a part of something so magical. It was no wonder the gardens had become a tourist attraction for the world and a competition among the staff. Only the best stayed on for the next gardening season. Only the best worked for Julian Carlton.

"Elizabeth! Why are you so quiet?" Madison had asked, sitting up straight to get a look into Elizabeth's eyes. It had always been a little joke between them, "the eyes never lie."

Madison had learned this lesson the hard way many years ago. As well behaved as she was, Madison had tried, like every child, to get away with murder. And she often did, her father too blinded by her hugs and kisses to ever see a fault in his only daughter's antics. But Elizabeth had always known. One look into her big, blue eyes and all guilt managed to reveal itself.

Madison looked into her friend's eyes for the truth.

"Ah, Madison, I was just thinking about what you said. You are right, this number, twenty-one. It is not what will make Madison; it is just that, a number. Who you are today, on the inside, is who you will be tomorrow, I promise. You have grown into a beautiful woman and your papa wants to show you off. There is nothing to be frightened of. It is a birthday party for you, like every year, just a little bigger and brighter than the rest, that's all."

Madison looked on with wide eyes, still unconvinced that she had nothing to be nervous about. Something deep inside gnawed at her, making it impossible to believe that after she turned twenty-one anything would be the same ever again. The extent to which her parents had gone to to organize this party and the obvious joy in her father's eyes as he looked at her lately sent off warning bells in Madison's head. Becoming an adult in the Carlton household was never just that simple, she knew. She looked into Elizabeth's eyes and wanted to fold herself into her arms and stay there, safe and content, forever. She wanted, desperately, to believe what her old friend was promising.

"Madison, what is it that scares you the most? Hmm? Is it all the people?" Elizabeth asked, pretending to air-kiss both cheeks the way she had seen the women from the surrounding mansions do so often.

"You are most used to this, what else? All the attention?" she asked, pretending to snap pictures of Madison with an imaginary camera.

"Well, you are very most used to this. And all the delicious food?" she asked finally, lightly pinching the soft flesh that bulged from her own round waist. "I for one still can't get used to that!"

They laughed and Madison threw herself back into Elizabeth's lap, relieved. She had always known just what to say to calm Madison's nerves. All the reassurance she ever needed lay in the deep lines of Elizabeth's smiling face and Madison suddenly knew that she could handle whatever the following days held for her. At that precious moment, nothing could have been more right in Madison's world.

Chapter Three

Each summer, the Carltons hired a staff of twelve to keep the lands specially tended and stunningly flourished all summer long. It was one of the family's greatest achievements and their most rewarding task.

Visitors from all over the world came to witness the truly spectacular gardens and fruit orchards for themselves after reading of their beauty in one magazine article or another. Their breathtaking gardens were famous worldwide, and for good reason.

Only the best in the field had been selected from hundreds of applicants every year. Hardworking men and women with a passion for their work come to the estate in hopes of working in the Carlton gardens or even just catching a glimpse of the family's beautiful daughter, Madison. For Madison was also famous around the world, known for her generosity and goodwill toward just about anyone who needed it.

It was, as most things, a Carlton tradition to keep the grounds in such immaculate order and groomed beauty. Julian had inherited the vision from his father and when the time came for him to head the household, he had insisted on continuing the tradition. He had even expanded the gardens and orchards in tribute to his late father.

Julian's pride lay in the success of his grounds and though he had no male successor, Madison would soon inherit the glory of this Carlton family tradition as well. After the announcement at the party, Madison would have more than just twenty-one years to celebrate and Julian was finding it hard to contain his excitement as he thought of all that the future held for his daughter.

"All is running smoothly I presume, Elizabeth?" Julian asked as he surveyed the progress of the preparations in the grand hall. He smoothed a napkin twice before shaking it free of its crease and refolding it. The tight nerves in his hands were as evident as the utter joy in his eyes.

"Ah sir, it is all coming together so nicely. It is as though tonight had been planned by the very gods who sent us our sweet Madison," she answered from the mantle, continuing to dust, all the while watching Julian through the antique mirror which hung above the wide fireplace.

Julian moved with new energy from the

table to one of the wall tapestries. He reached out for a moment and felt the thick fabric, detailed and elegant in design, between his fingers before centering it to a perfect symmetry with all the others.

"Yes, Elizabeth, I agree. Everything looks perfect. I've been waiting for this celebration since the night Victoria placed my little girl in my arms. I knew she was special, that very night I knew it. Her enormous eyes were already bright and alert staring up at me. I'll never forget the way she looked at me, as though we weren't strangers at all, as though we were old friends, her and I.

"My little angel. That is what I used to call her. Do you remember, Elizabeth? It was her nickname and she made good on it too. She is an angel. She has made her mother and me so proud." He stopped to survey the position of the dessert carousels.

"Yes sir. We are all very proud of her. She was a darling babe, always one step ahead, a smart babe she was. I always knew she would inherit the Carlton brilliance. And the beauty, sir. I swear I see your mother's face every time I look at her. Stopped my heart more than once, sir."

Elizabeth continued her work, enjoying the opportunity to reminisce with Julian. She had served his parents when he was a young boy. He was always bouncing around the mansion, she remembered, and never could sit still. She looked back at him now. He had grown to be a wonderful man, husband and father. He was so strong and proud and honorable and at that moment, Elizabeth saw the same little boy from so many years ago. Her heart broke silently and she blinked a tear away.

Julian inched a water glass to the right and then finally spoke with obvious strain. "Just twenty years ago, my God, Elizabeth, where have the years gone?"

He caught a glimpse of his aged hands and stepped back, momentarily alarmed by the sight of them. More and more he was beginning to see his father's reflection stare back at him in the mirror. Age had crept up on him somehow and years had slipped happily away.

Julian paused a while to regain composure before continuing. "I never imagined time would disappear like it has . . ." His voice trailed off as he stared up at the massive chandelier, appearing to be inspecting it for dust, though Elizabeth knew he wasn't inspecting at all.

Julian was a thoughtful man, sensitive to his emotions as well as to the thoughts and feeling of others. She knew he was lost in thought now, dreaming of earlier days when he was a younger man and Madison was still his little baby girl.

He drew a deep breath, pulled back his broad shoulders and turned to leave. "Please, Elizabeth, if there are any problems will you come to me first? I don't want Victoria disturbed today."

His voice faded as he had already crossed the room to leave before he could finish his request. His intentions were as sincere as ever, though his mind was clearly elsewhere.

"Of course, my child," she said to herself and wiped a stray tear from her own cheek.

Chapter Four

Victoria Carlton knocked gently on the thick oak door before pushing it open and peering into her husband's quarters. Finding Julian warming by the large hearth, Victoria simply leaned silently against the door frame and beheld him. He hadn't heard her knock.

He was seated in an oversized leather armchair, glasses perched on the end of his nose, a classic fiction of some kind at his knee. He was undeniably the most charming man she had ever known and she took these few precious moments to stare at her greatest love.

Most days Victoria was preoccupied, distracted by her anger and pain but today was actually okay, today would be considered a good day. Julian seemed to be doing better than ever and she suspected she knew why. Madison's twenty-first birthday was significant to both of them. As her parents, they were proud and thrilled for her and, as the current heads of the Carlton Mansion, they were confident and assured in their decisions for the family's future.

Victoria felt her long, slender body relax at the sight of her husband's calm. She enjoyed watching the slow, steady rise and fall of his chest, the glint of his blue eyes as they read line after line.

That morning, in the privacy of their quarters, she wore only a silk day coat. The delicate fabric clung to her thin frame and was pulled tightly around her tiny waist, revealing her feminine shape. The pastel violet color accentuated the rosy hue of her perfect skin. The coat's collar hung loose around her neck and shoulders and her long, dark hair was swept up off her back. Shorter strands escaped the French twist and framed her small chin. Defiant waves fell around her mysterious eyes and she left them there, as was her habit to hide behind her luxurious hair.

Victoria had been very young when she married Julian, only twenty. Yet, so had all the other Carlton women. Tradition, she would soon find out, was the Carlton way, the only way. He had been older, ten years older, and more experienced. But it wasn't just the marriage arrangement Victoria and Julian had fulfilled on their wedding day, it was their undying love for each other. Love at first sight is how she often described it and nothing could have been more accurate.

Looking at him now, she realized that the love had only multiplied over the years. How lucky she was, to be loved by such a man and to have served him well with such a brilliant and dazzling daughter. She would be selfish now and steal a few more moments before she disturbed him.

Sadly, it seemed like that was all they had left now, stolen moments and manipulated calm. They were so busy entertaining during the year and this year was even busier. Madison would be coming of age in a few short hours and then nothing would be the same again, Victoria knew. And she could tell her husband's body was slowing down even though his spirit refused to. She wasn't sure how much time they had left together — years, months, days. Nobody had ever been sure or able to give an accurate estimate, but all of a sudden it wasn't enough.

She wanted forever. Victoria wanted to be old and done with life herself when her husband died, not middle-aged and still aching to be loved each and every day as she had been all these glorious years. It wasn't fair. Victoria knew life wouldn't be fair for her or her daughter once Julian left them.

The clatter of plates could be heard from

downstairs and Elizabeth's voice rose strong above the others as she gave orders to those scurrying past in their rush to complete the appointed tasks.

A smile crept over Victoria's full lips. Reality swept over her and she remembered again that it was a good day. Her baby was twenty-one and finally a woman. Joy and pain filled her heart and a single tear escaped her closed eyes.

Victoria had held her family so close only to realize that they didn't belong to her. They belonged to the world. They were everyone's husband, daughter, family.

She had learned to accept their social position early on and though it was hard, Victoria made the best of it on every occasion. But she still longed to have just one thing for themselves, just one birthday alone, just one celebration to themselves.

It would not be so. Madison was twenty-one, not just for her friends and family, but for the entire community who had anticipated and monitored her maturity and introduction into the social circle since birth. And soon to follow, an elaborate wedding that would also showcase their perfect little family to the world. Yes, this year would be busier than ever. Victoria knew Madison would soon belong to a suitable man and she hoped that her daughter would someday even grow to love him.

She bit her tears back and focused on Julian. She would be strong and protect everything he no longer could — tradition, family, reputation, stature. He was growing weak, she noticed, despite his high spirits. It wouldn't be long now. A chill ran through her as she took the vow. Victoria would do whatever was needed to protect herself and her daughter's future as well as the Carlton name. Anything.

"Darling?" she whispered finally, as not to startle him.

Julian smiled before he looked up and then stared a while before he asked, "Are you cold, my love? Please come in and join me by the fire. Elizabeth has brought me this throw. I just can't seem to get warmed either. There must be a draft in the house. Please remind me to speak with Joseph about it." He held out a hand and gestured for her to join him.

He removed his glasses, closed his novel and set them both aside. He smoothed his large hands over the heavy fabric and gave his wife his full attention. His brows were knit together in concentration and Victoria was reminded again of his brilliant mind. She had always known that when his body began to fail his mind would remain vital and strong. It was a fate as cruel to him as it was kind to his family.

Victoria crossed the room to him, her stride elegant and sure. She was a truly striking woman, particularly to her husband. Even after all these years, he still marveled at her beauty and grace.

"Here, darling, let me help you." She pulled the throw higher on his thighs and seated herself on the arm of his chair. Taking his head in her hands, she kissed his forehead.

"No, I'm not chilled and there certainly is no draft. Why, it's almost June. I was just thinking there at the door while I watched you read. What I am worried about is you, darling. Let me ring Elizabeth for some hot tea." She rose to see to it.

"No, no, I'm fine now that you are here with me. Besides, I'd rather not interrupt the preparations." He reached up and rubbed her shoulder gently, letting his hand slide down to the small of her back, where he left it for a moment.

"Yes, the preparations," she whispered, staring off into the fire as her mind journeyed back to the sea of memories that seemed to rise up and engulf her a million times a day.

Julian stared up at his wife and wondered about the dreamy look in her dark eyes. His stare swept from the sharp slant of her mysterious eyes to the delicate curve of her jaw.

"God, you are beautiful." His hand firmly guided her back down to the arm of his chair and then slid up her straight back to her neck. It was his favorite part on her, so soft and sexy. He could get a giggle out of her with one faint stroke of his fingers on the delicate skin there.

She felt his strong hand on her neck and slowly melted from the warmth of it. She leaned into him and pressed her lips to his. Aware that her silk coat had come open, she fell further into his embrace, warmed and delighted. He was still so strong, so alive with desire for her . . .

How could it be?

How would she go on without him?

How could there be life without this? After this?

His mouth rose to hers. He lightly kissed the deep corners and the wonderful little space between her bottom lip and chin. He moved across her face, lightly, kissing every inch, softly, brushing his lips across her thin eyelids, her thick lashes and up further to her arched brows as his steady hand explored her. Julian felt a new strength come over his body as he held his wife. He felt the familiar ache of his undying desire for her wash over him.

He had fallen in love the minute his eyes had beheld her. Her dark hair served as a jolt of energy through his body the instant she removed her shawl. Twenty-two years ago, Julian's large, blue eyes met Victoria's dark, mysterious stare and they had both known. Julian had immediately thanked his father for the arrangement of their wedding.

"But are you sure she is a suitable wife, son? We feel she is right for you, but do you feel the same? After all, Julian, you have only had one meeting with the girl. How could you possibly know so soon?"

Julian had only answered, "I love her," and it was final. The two were wed the following month in the grand hall of the Carlton Mansion, where his mother and grandmother had been wed and his daughter would be too.

Now, so many years later, the energy, the passion between Julian and Victoria had remained strong. A life of love, passion and tradition is what Julian had led. And now, the pride of his daughter's birthday followed by her union to Arthur, heir of the Leemon fortune, was everything he had dreamt of. His daughter would soon find love and passion and fortune in the man he had chosen for her. It was all she deserved and everything he now lived for.

Chapter Five

Madison stood staring at her reflection in the mirror. She was barefoot and nude, save the silk pajama pants and lace bra she wore that morning. Her hair was pulled loosely into a high ponytail atop her head, revealing her clear complexion and even clearer ocean-blue eyes.

It was the morning of her twenty-first birthday and a busy grooming schedule awaited her but she was in no rush to invite her hairstylist and makeup artist into her dressing-room just yet. She needed to soak up the calming solitude a while longer before she invited the chaos in.

The strap of her bra fell as she watched herself move in the mirror that hung above her vanity. Her glance shifted from her slim figure to a picture encased in a diamond and platinum-encrusted frame hanging a few inches to the right.

She had been sixteen when the portrait was taken and she could remember everything about the day, including the party that had followed in the evening. She stepped closer to it for a moment and noted the bright eyes and long eyelashes that stared back at her, the plump mouth and smooth skin. Madison reached out and traced an index finger along the lines in the photograph and tried to remember more.

Had she been as nervous that day as she felt now? Had she looked forward to the day and the year that followed?

She pressed her eyes closed and when she let them flutter open again, her stare shifted back into the mirror and she looked deeper into the reflection. High, round cheekbones were more evident now and the thin layer of baby fat around her jaw-line was diminishing. Perfectly shaped eyebrows were arching more and more dramatically each day. Her neck was slimmer and the long, tight muscles in her shoulders were faintly noticeable under her skin. She frowned purposefully and regarded the creases that formed in her brow and nose. Once she released the scowl, the lines disappeared.

Twenty-one. She had looked forward to the number — the age — for so long and now it had finally taken effect.

Madison turned from the mirror and thought of the differences between childhood and adulthood. There had seemed so many for so long but now that she was faced with the reality, it seemed there were actually very few differences to count. She had always, as early as she could remember, been expected to study hard and act respectfully and maturely. She had also predominately socialized with adults or young people who behaved as maturely and sophisticated as she did.

Madison wondered what exactly would change after tonight. She remembered that college would be ending soon. That would be a drastic change, she realized sadly and yet she was excited about starting the life she had envisioned for herself. She and an acquaintance from school had great plans to put some of the mass riches they knew the world possessed to good use and make a difference where it was needed most. She had always enjoyed the comfort she was granted but she also believed she couldn't enjoyably go on into her adulthood unless she also worked to enable others to experience the same opportunities she had been given. Ideas began to swim in her head about the future and she had to remind herself that she had to get through this evening first.

The gown she was to wear that night hung stiffly on the Judy that Elizabeth had wheeled in that morning. The mannequin was an exact replica of Madison's current measurements so most of the many fittings could be done without her presence. At noon she would have had the final fitting and by then the gown would mold perfectly to her body, as though sculpted or painted on by an artist. Crystal-heeled shoes stood on a pedestal beside the gown and a sparkling tiara sat in a glass box below them.

Madison could imagine the process in her mind. She had gone through it countless times yet the excitement and fun of dressing up never dimmed. With Elizabeth by her side and a few other professionals, she would be transformed from the clean, natural beauty that stared back at her now into a glamorous woman. And tonight, it was finally official. Tonight she *was* a woman.

Chapter Six

Cars lined the streets surrounding the Carlton Mansion on the afternoon of the celebration.

Hired security had Carlton Lane sectioned off and closed by six o'clock that morning. All catering trucks and staff were instructed to use the back entrance and service streets to access the mansion.

Six suited police officers were now positioned outside the various entrances, working efficiently to approve all cars approaching the grounds. Once they were approved by security, each car was waved in and inched up to join the line-up of extravagant cars that were waiting to be valet parked.

By five o'clock, the guest garages were full and locked for the night. Now, valets hurried to greet those who drove up the grand driveway in long limousines while hosts chauffeured guests arriving by car and driver through the second entrance.

The scene was inspiring as unseen photographers took this opportunity to observe the richest, most glamorous people in Long Island. Shutters clicked as their cameras captured the arriving guests through long-zoomed lenses. They would photograph as much as they could from the perimeter of the mansion and deliver exactly what the public wanted by morning.

Ladies with long, sweeping gowns and sparkling diamond jewels at their wrists and throats held the arms of gentlemen in black suits and ties. Each donned a smile on their lips as they climbed the marble steps of the mansion's grand entrance.

Glittering cufflinks disappeared into suit pockets, each emerging with a personal, handcrafted gold card which had been sent and received, along with two hundred other specially selected invitations, three months prior to this evening.

Couples lined the grand staircase as they waited to present their invitations a second time to the tight security. Freshly manicured fingers pulled stole wraps up over bare shoulders though the spring evening air was already thick and moist with humidity.

The hall was loud as the orchestra played a quick waltz to welcome the new guests. Laughter could be heard as it rose and fell among the many conversations between guests and old friends.

The Carlton parties were a tradition as much as they were a public service. The households of the surrounding estates were lifelong friends, heirs of the families who had established them centuries ago, and socializing among the elite community of estates was certainly a priority seldom fulfilled.

The Carlton household remedied that.

Julian and Victoria committed to throwing a grand ball annually in celebration of their friends and family. Tonight, though, was an extraordinary celebration, an event so dear to the Carlton family that it would also be shared by everyone close to them. Madison, in all her glory, would be celebrated this very night.

Julian watched the magnificent scene, unnoticed and thoughtful, from his private bedroom balcony, which overlooked the grand hall.

He stood awed by the sight before him and was touched deep in his heart. The hall had filled considerably and he was pleased with the progress of the celebration so far yet it was the laughter and festivity on his friends' faces that sent his heart soaring.

He turned as Victoria entered his

chamber. He had often felt her presence seeking him out before she actually materialized.

She had taken the afternoon to pamper and dress and the results were outstanding. Victoria stood before her husband in a deep royal blue, velvet gown. It was a designer strapless that formed to every movement and accentuated every curve of her long, thin frame.

Her hair was stylishly pulled back tightly to the nape of her neck, where the thick strands were held by an exquisite diamond clasp, the center sparkled with tiny sapphires. Her dark curls spouted rebelliously from the hold and cascaded down her bare back in sensual, loose spirals.

Victoria went to him without a word. She had seen the look come over her husband's face as his eyes swept over her. His eyes sparkled with pride and delight; they never could hide a single thing. He was pleased with her and she grew an even greater confidence from his approval. She had long since gotten past the shyness she once suffered as a young girl and threw her bare shoulders back in response to his stare. And when she finally raised her chin to him, her gaze bore deep into his eyes. Yes, he was definitely pleased with her. All she had ever needed to know lay bare in the blueness of his eyes.

"I like your hair off your pretty face. I can see your eyes." He held her delicate face in his hands and brought his to hers to look deeper.

"Still don't see the end in them though. I think they may go on for centuries." He searched with an air of mischief and youth on his lips, anticipating the night ahead and wanting only to hold her in his arms and dance the night away.

"Layers and layers, just like my sweet Victoria." He kissed her blackened lashes.

Her eyes were as mysterious to him as she was. So quiet and content she always seemed, and he had often wondered what went on in her gorgeous head. She could hide pain and suffering behind those layers. That was something he had learned about her soon after they were married. His eyes, on the contrary, were as clear as the morning sky, revealing every emotion whether he intended to or not. He couldn't help worrying about her now and again. She could hide her pain well and he just couldn't stand the thought of her ever being hurt.

"Sweet Julian." She leaned into him, grateful for the few moments alone. "How are you feeling this evening?"

She had asked this question for years out of courtesy, but ever since the disturbing news she had received two years ago she now asked out of deep concern.

Diverting her face from his so he wouldn't see the pain in it, she asked again, "Please, darling, how do you feel?"

"Wonderful," Julian whispered into her decorated ear, taking a deep breath of her scent.

He would never worry his wife with the truth. He hadn't slept at all that morning. As a matter of fact, he hadn't really slept in weeks. Anyway, he thought, it was probably just nerves.

"I'm glad to hear it. Now, are you ready?"

It was time to put on a brave face. The guests awaited Victoria and Julian's entrance. They could forget their troubles for tonight, for their friends and family, and for Madison, always for their dear Madison.

Chapter Seven

Couples swirled in dizzy circles to the warm hum of the orchestra. Guests had spilled out onto the hall's balcony, carrying with them the soft sounds of music and laughter into the night's breeze.

Looking out over the property was magical; the gardens absolutely glowed against the blackened night. Many stood mesmerized by the sight, and the feeling. Between the laughter and the music and the champagne, everything seemed to slow until it felt time would almost stop completely. And many wished it would; no one wanted the night to end and all would regretfully say goodnight when it was all over.

The chatter was loud inside the hall as excitement grew among the guests. Staff circled the busy floor, offering fresh wine and hors d'oeuvres and clearing up empty plates and glasses.

Elizabeth manned the kitchen, assembling serving trays for the floor crew, not because she was needed or had to but because she wanted to and loved to. She loved being a part of the hustle and bustle and somehow felt closer to the family she served by seeing to every detail herself. She stepped out into the ballroom only to tend to the needs of Julian and Victoria.

The handsome pair entered arm in arm, with the poise of a truly exquisite couple. Welcoming the crowd with warm embraces, Julian and Victoria gained the attention of every guest in the hall as old friends became new again.

This commotion continued until each cheek was kissed and every hand was shook. The welcoming tradition was very personal and thorough. Though the hall was full with hundreds of guests, each received personal attention from the host and hostess. It was tradition.

When all had been greeted, Julian and Victoria finally took their place at the antique podium stationed before the grand fireplace. The lectern was a family heirloom that was frequently taken down from the study temporarily and used for toasts, and this evening there would be many.

Julian motioned for Elizabeth's attention as he announced to his wife, "It is time."

"Elizabeth, send for my daughter please."

By the time Elizabeth finally managed to

soothe Madison's nerves and get her downstairs, the entire room was buzzing with anticipation. Madison was seldom in attendance at the parties her parents threw and many were excited to finally see her in person and all grown up.

Madison entered the hall with the stance of a goddess, confident, yet humble. Her beautiful lips curled up into a beaming smile and her absolute happiness radiated from her eyes. Her gown was a startling midnight black and her jewelry consisted of endless rows of sparkling diamonds at her throat and wrists. Her milky white skin glowed against the black satin and her golden hair curled sweetly around the sparkling white gold and diamond tiara.

All servers halted to acknowledge Madison's arrival and the crowd quickly quieted without cue. Dozens came in from the terrace to get a better look at her as the orchestra hummed lightly.

Every woman looked on in envy at the magnificent sight, secretly coveting Madison's soft skin and shiny golden hair. Every man in the hall watched the sleek line of her leg, ankle to thigh, and the supple moisture in her reddened lips. Madison was the sight every woman defined as classic beauty and the one every man locked in memory for their private fantasies. She was the perfect picture of youth, innocence and charm. Madison was perfect.

The crowd had held their breath as their eyes beheld the entrance and a shy hand went up to her bodice as Madison observed the crowd's reaction. A roaring applause broke out once everyone caught their breath.

Madison reached to her left for her old friend's hand. Finding it nowhere within grasp, she stood alone before the hundreds of people she hardly knew, while her parents beamed with pride.

"I would like to introduce my beautiful daughter," Julian began. "Madison Carlton. Tonight we celebrate her twenty-first birthday and so much more."

Chapter Eight

Tears welled up in Madison's blue eyes. She blinked hard, forcing them back, saving them for someplace else, and she swallowed sharply.

Married to Arthur of the Leemon fortune? Was she thrilled or appalled? It was a fine line between the two. She didn't even *know* Arthur.

Sure, he was handsome and gentle and everything a debutant could wish for, but Madison had thought she was different, a modern and contemporary woman and certainly not a candidate for the next Carlton tradition.

And though a million thoughts were running rampant through her head, she forced a smile in her parents' direction and then toward all the guests who stood staring, champagne raised high.

"A toast everyone, to my daughter Madison." Julian concluded his speech at his daughter's smile and two hundred glasses clanged in a toast to Madison's birthday and soon-to-be wedding.

"Look darling, our daughter sheds tears of joy. Arthur will make her very happy," Julian whispered proudly to Victoria, who nodded in response.

Victoria's stare narrowed on her daughter's eyes. Clear as her father's, and Victoria could see it all. Madison was in turmoil. Thank God she had gone along with the announcement and hadn't made a scene at the shocking news.

Victoria knew her daughter would be devastated at the arrangement. Such traditions did not apply to the young lady who could change the world with her smile. College and traveling to exotic places with girlfriends were what young, beautiful women cared about at twenty-one years of age, not wedding plans and babies or mergers. But how could she, or anyone else, break Carlton tradition or Julian's heart?

Yes, Madison would go along with the arrangement and, in time, she would learn to give up her dreams. She would learn to love Arthur Leemon.

The applause grew louder as Julian announced the lucky bachelor and shook hands with his parents; everyone approved of the union. The Carltons had chosen well.

"Arthur will have his own practice next

year," many announced knowingly. "Aren't you excited, sweetie?"

But Madison only felt nauseated and gulped down her flute of champagne. "I beg your pardon?" she asked one spectacularly ornamented lady in particular. Everything seemed to slow and the scene around her scattered into fragments before her eyes. It was as if everyone had acquired a new language that she just couldn't understand.

"The engagement, the wedding. Aren't you absolutely thrilled, young lady?" she asked suspiciously. If Madison didn't want Arthur she had plenty of granddaughters who would.

"The engagement, right, of course. It will be magnificent," Madison managed and the lady seemed satisfied with her answer.

Somewhere, Arthur rose and managed to negotiate the crowd until he was by Madison's trembling side. Obliging the crowd, he quickly pecked her flushed cheeks.

A crowd formed as every male guest lined up to shake Arthur's lucky hand. He had won the prize and was the envy of all who had tried, come close, but failed.

Madison dared a quick glance at her new fiancé. Excitement sparkled in his eyes and she wanted to scream. Sure, they had spoken a few words to each other, engaged in polite conversation during dinner parties, but forever with this man?

How could her parents do this to her? Without warning or concern for her feelings? They had made a decision that would change the rest of her life and had announced it to the world before informing her first. Her stare went from the mysterious face of her mother to her proud father's and back to Arthur's illicit delirium.

She fought back the hot, liquid anger that threatened to erupt from her while all the laughter and chatting meshed around her. If this was such an honor then why did she feel so betrayed? Hadn't she known this was coming? Somewhere, deep in her subconscious, she had known it was only a matter of time before she was expected to marry and assume the responsibility that accompanied adulthood in the Carlton family.

Yes, of course she had known. So why had she not prepared herself for this very moment. Twenty-one years had been given to her to prepare and yet here she was, shocked and overcome with the kind of emotions she could have never anticipated feeling. Every ounce of logic still left in her urged her to be happy, for herself, for her parents and for the Leemons, yet her heart and soul, an overwhelming combination, screamed and throbbed horribly with the pain of a deep, raw cut.

Tradition. She wanted to purge the word from her mind, from her realm of understanding, from her soul.

And just as Arthur was surrounded and praised, now too was Madison. They all spoke at once, pulling this way and that.

"When do you think you'll have it, spring or fall?"

"Have you chosen a color scheme? It is the most important part you know —"

"How exciting! Silk or satin?"

"Where is he taking you for the honeymoon, honey?"

The smiling faces blurred and distorted before Madison's eyes. Tears, fear and champagne clouded her sight and the orchestra played a thousand times faster, over and over in her head. Her body was numb and clumsy as the women hugged and kissed her, patting her arms, her legs, her soft golden curls.

The room swam and voices blurred. Julian and Victoria waved at her and toasted with the Leemons once more and then a voice rose above the rest. "Madison, are you all right?"

"Elizabeth," she answered faintly before falling back against a dessert carousel.

Cream puffs and chocolate éclairs scattered the floor and powdered sugar tinted the air a soft white, making it all look like what Madison wanted it to be — just a dream.

She regained her footing almost as quickly as she had lost it and when she faced the crowd again, all the faces had turned concerned and confused. They reached out to her in concern but Madison pushed through them all, lurching across the ballroom and out the French doors. All she heard was Elizabeth's frantic voice among the sweet waltz that continued to play, mocking her with its joyful tune.

Out at last, she breathed deeply, sucking in the moisture of the night's humidity. She leaned far over the balcony and tried to cool herself. When she thought she was finally calm enough, she looked back into the hall through tears that perpetually spilled.

The dining room stood almost still now as the guests consulted each other about what had happened. Many of those who had witnessed the whole thing were enchanted with the spectacle of the blushing bride and rushed to the French doors to see what Madison would do next.

She had to escape; she had to leave all this commotion and for the first time she didn't care what anyone thought.

Her parents toasted again, somewhere deep inside the hall, while Arthur continued well on his way to a drunken state of celebratory bliss. And just as quickly as they had become interested, many of the guests now grew bored with Madison's disturbance. Mercifully, more champagne was being circulated. Everyone wanted another glass and another waltz on the marble dance floor before the party wound down. Only Elizabeth fought through the fickle crowd until she was at the glass doors and scanning the terrace for Madison.

Their eyes met for a brief moment and in that instant, Elizabeth's heart was violently punctured.

"Madison! Come back!" Elizabeth called out but her voice was lost in the enormous crowd.

Madison turned her face away from her old friend and without a word headed down the terrace's moonlit steps and dashed into the garden, leaving the party — *her* party, she thought bitterly — merely a faint hum in the distance.

She had never before been beyond the terrace this late at night but she had to go; it seemed to call out to her. And the deeper and deeper she went into the gardens, the farther they invited her in.

Chapter Nine

Johnny lay back on his elbows and let his head fall back until the thick grass combed through his shaggy strands.

Perfect, he thought.

Since the day he had arrived at the Carlton Estate, he had worked the grass with special care while others merely maintained it. He had tended and pored over it as passionately as he did his sketches, passionately and protectively. He'd even found himself quoting his father in an attempt to inspire the other workers: "Grass is just as important as the flowers and trees, probably more so. It is the canvas you begin your masterpiece on."

No use. They hardly noticed he was around let alone that he was a genius. One day they'll see, all of them, he vowed.

Johnny did have to admit his own surprise at the grass's color and thickness. It was remarkable how it had regained its vibrancy so soon after the long, cold winter and had flourished with so little attention. It down right baffled him, as did so many other things since his arrival on this strange land, like the ancient oaks and giant fruits that grew in the orchards. But mostly, Johnny wondered when he was going to get an eyeful of Madison Carlton.

Raising his head and his thick brows now, he stared off towards the mansion and listened to the faint music. He chuckled to himself as the garden and terrace lights blurred with each gulp of his cheap beer.

For a summer job, Johnny had found himself in heaven. Doing what he was good at and working on the world famous Carlton acres had Johnny pulling weeds with a smile. A new life and the chance of a lifetime were long overdue for this twenty-five-year-old starving artist. Spending more than half his life nursing a dream and a sick father, Johnny was ready for a brand new life. And this was it. This was what it was like to have it all. He looked on and knew, one day, he too would have it all — but on his own terms.

No fake galas to show off the goods. Johnny saw through the lacquered hair and nails and what he saw disgusted him. Cramming preppy frat jerks into expensive suits and shiny shoes never made anyone a man. And prettying up girls to sell off into money and supposed happiness never made anyone really happy.

Johnny just couldn't believe that these families still operated that way. In fact, he hadn't even thought of it until his site manager, Kay, had sat him down the first day to lay down the ground rules. And there were many. Workers weren't even allowed to give a "Hey, what's up?" to the old employers.

But Johnny didn't concern himself with that, all he really wanted was to do his job and get on with his life. New place, new life, new opportunities, and he knew he was lucky to have this one. Though he prided himself on bashing their ways, Johnny had to admit that it felt good to be a part of something again. The Carlton Mansion awed him as much as it boiled his blood. And he couldn't wait to get a good look at the family who could afford all the majesty that surrounded him. If he didn't respect their traditions, he most certainly respected their quality of life.

Chapter Ten

Madison tore down the stony walkway and veered off the path when she looked back and could still see the looming mansion behind her.

Slowing now, unsure of how long she'd been running and how far she'd gone, she finally stopped before one of the orchard's iron archways. The dark metal was nearly covered as lush, green ivy climbed and wound itself tight and securely around it. And though the vines clung to its sturdy metal foundation, she noticed, the leaves continued to climb and reach up towards the sky.

Exhausted and much calmer now, Madison dropped down on the soft grass and continued to stare up at the arch while she tried to clear her head and think. She no longer heaved and wiped at her wet face. She just sat and let her breath deepen, allowing the tears to spill over her burning cheeks.

And that's how he found her.

Something had scooted by him so fast he

was almost certain it was just a raccoon making off with some party favors.

Though he didn't remember getting himself up off the grass, he did remember following the scent of lilacs and the soft golden glow that illuminated the way. And here she was, breathtaking, though it appeared she had had quite a night.

Could this actually be who he thought it was? Johnny had never seen anything more beautiful and he knew that it was her.

"I always knew I was a good crewman, sweetheart, but I never expected this kind of praise. Sheesh, it's just some climbing ivy. You don't have to get so emotional."

She had heard it, his deep soothing voice. A dream? She couldn't tell; she didn't care to tell. She just sat, alone, and nothing else existed.

The little bumps on her arms from the cooling night air, the sparkling tiara that half hung off a golden curl and the deep, young voice behind her . . . none of it existed.

Madison roused with the cold night on her face. Everything now felt like a different place and time. An old nightmare resurfaced, one where the night had been hot and suffocating and she had been running and running.

Breathing deeply, Madison felt the coolness soothe the burning. She stirred and stretched the tight muscles in her arms and legs.

Her body, she realized, swam in an oversized, cotton sweater. Her arms were draped over in long sleeves and her searching fingers were lost in the endless fabric.

Dreamy and confused, she heard it again, that voice, so familiar. It was so very odd that it didn't startle her as it didn't take much to make her jump.

"Hi, beautiful. You gonna let me see those crystal blues? Come on, look right in mine now," cooed the familiar and impossibly deep voice.

"Where am I?" Madison asked, rubbing her aching head with a cotton covered fist.

"Now that's better, darling. A little color and consciousness looks good on you, so let's keep it that way, okay? Sit up and have a look around, though you're cute when you're confused." He was amused now that his goddess was awake, but he had been enchanted all night as she slept soundlessly in his arms.

Madison tried to clear her head while she looked around. She was wearing a man's sweater and appeared to be curled up in the owner's lap. They sat together on a discreet bench beside the pond, much, much farther than she'd ever been alone at night. But she wasn't alone. Though she didn't even know this man and had barely gotten a look at him, still, she felt safe and anything but alone. More like warm and cozy against the night's air.

She hardly noticed the throb of her head and the ache in her limbs when she finally looked into his eyes.

Ah, there you are, her own voice whispered in her head.

"How do you feel?" His light brown eyes searched her face, concerned and waiting. She almost fell into his endless stare and then caught herself.

"Fine. Sleeping on strange men in my father's garden is one of my favorite pastimes," she answered tartly.

He ignored the sarcasm oozing from her tone and sat back, comfortable now that her highness was obviously feeling more like herself.

"Good. Do you come here often? It's really beautiful here by the water." He'd try her again, give her one more chance before he would decide if he liked her better unconscious.

Amazing, she thought, is he just slow or incredibly smart? She'd soon find out. "No, actually I don't dwell much in the outdoors.

With all the sun and vegetation and fresh air, I fear I may become less princess-like." She gave him an exaggerated batting of her big blue eyes.

"Actually, you're right. You do sort of look like a horror-movie prom queen. We better get you inside and quick." He waited a beat then let out the amusement that tickled his throat. He had seen her expression change from smug to shocked and finally, deeply offended.

Yes, they would defiantly get along, even when she was conscious. She sat, arms crossed over her chest, ignoring him and he couldn't have been more pleased.

"Okay, honey, lose the attitude. We're just playing here. It isn't all that bad, a little paint thinner and we'll have that mascara off your cheeks in no time."

That finally managed to get the reaction he was looking for. She lunged, fury flashing through the icy blue of her eyes. He caught her wrists just in time since he had been expecting a little action after the stunt he had just pulled.

Managing to pin her hands back behind her was easier once she broke out in laughter, collapsing against his restrain.

"Ah, there it is, exactly what you needed. Now I suppose you feel better?"

"Much," she replied and this time he wiped the large rolling tears from her smiling face.

"How is she?" Joseph asked his wife as she silently slid into bed at 4:30 A.M.

"Ah, better now that she's fallen asleep. Rest yourself; we've got cleanup tomorrow."

"Yes, we've all got much to do getting things back to the ordinary around here. Though there's not much point as we'll be setting up for a wedding just as soon as we've cleaned up. I do hope that sweet thing is feeling better." Joseph yawned and snuggled into his wife's back for a couple hours of sleep.

"Too much pressure on the thing, didn't I try to tell them? You raise a babe, you are sure going to know the thing better than you know yourself. Even better than that babe would like you knowing about 'em."

Elizabeth tried her best to settle in, for her husband's sake. The truth was, she had waited for Madison to come home after the episode at the party for hours. She had even gone out as far as the orchards in search of her. She had not returned to her room, or the mansion, Elizabeth suspected, all night.

Worry racked her still, though she had seen Madison head off into the gardens. She knew she would be safe there, but still she worried.

Elizabeth slipped her fingers around the rosary she kept under her pillow and prayed the gardens would heal Madison's broken heart. The news of an engagement had certainly been a shock to all of them but she had to admit that it was hardly a surprise.

Elizabeth had known that this day would come; she just hadn't expected it to be this soon. Elizabeth wondered now if she had done her job well and prepared Madison for what she needed to do next. She could only watch and see and be there for Madison as she always had been.

Chapter Eleven

Meet me by the pond at seven.
And the name's Johnny —

Madison read the scribbled, handwritten note she found pinned to the hibiscus tree that sat on her balcony the next morning. She looked around guiltily. If anyone had seen . . . a risk taker, she decided she liked this Johnny already.

"Morning, Elizabeth." Madison breezed into the sunny kitchen where the old housekeeper was preparing a fantastic breakfast for the family.

Madison surveyed the assortment of fresh fruit and vegetables and couldn't help stealing a ripe, purple grape from the fruit salad.

"Glad to see you are feeling better. A day's rest is all you need when you're as young as you are." Elizabeth glanced up from the stove where she was preparing Julian's favorite breakfast, scrambled eggs, Belgium waffles and exotic fruit salad.

That famous smile was back on Madison's lips and something told her a night in the gardens and a day of rest weren't the only reasons for it.

"Have you seen father this morning?" Madison stole a slice of pineapple this time and Elizabeth pretended not to notice.

"Ah, yes, he sits on the patio reading today's news."

"Oh, you know that's just an excuse so he'll be first in line for your eggs."

"You are sweet this morning. Soon I will be preparing breakfast for you and your husband, serving eggs to Arthur out on the patio." Elizabeth smiled up at Madison casually and that was all she needed to see the truth in her eyes.

Madison felt the anxiety quickly come over her as freshly as the previous night when she first found out about the arrangement. The happy flutters that tickled her insides ever since she met the man — Johnny — in the garden now turned to sour pinches. She quickly hid the nausea that was growing in her stomach with a weak smile and headed out towards the patio without another word.

She found her father seated at the large iron table. The sight of him always awed her and the newspaper he poured over, she hoped, was the perfect distraction from her worries. Julian loved discussing and debating current events with his daughter.

His hair had grayed over the years and he had grown a little thin recently but he still remained the strongest, most dignified man Madison had ever known. She was proud to be part of this family, the roots and its traditions, even though she had doubted them more in the last thirty-six hours than ever before.

"Hi, Daddy, nice morning, isn't it?"

"Good morning, angel. I'm glad to see you up and around. Thought you might have been ill the way you disappeared after the party and shut yourself up all day yesterday. Elizabeth said it was just the thing for exhaustion. Looks like she was right, as usual. Too much excitement, hmm, angel?" Julian's blue eyes gleamed up at his daughter. "I worried it would be, but when I saw you the other night, so happy, I knew we had chosen well and that you thought so too."

He cleared the newspaper sections from the table and offered Madison a seat. "You will be so happy. Soon you will have a successful man beside you as you create your own family together, your own memories, while remembering the old together," he continued on mercilessly. All the while, Madison sat, fighting back the nausea with a smile, and nodded encouragingly as Julian slowly got to his point, "I thank God every night, Madison. Do you know why?" he asked and she nodded "no" fiercely. She hadn't seen this ambush coming.

"For you, for your mother, for all of this that I have, and I am thankful for Elizabeth. You know she's been here, with the Carltons, even before I was. So I guess Elizabeth is a tradition and I want you to carry that on as well. I want her there for your children's births just as she was there for mine and yours. There's something magical in that, tradition."

"Of course, Daddy, you know how I respect the family's tradition. And Elizabeth, well she's like a mother to me," Madison responded without missing a beat. Her response was as true as what her family had ingrained in her and for a minute, she believed every word she said.

"Good." Julian smiled and believed her too. "Now, where are those eggs?"

Chapter Twelve

Caught in one of his fantasies about what he'd do with the kind of money the Carltons had, Johnny sat back lazily on the same bench he had on the night of the party when he had held Madison beneath the same twinkling stars.

He hadn't heard her come up behind him on slow, cautious footsteps but he knew she was there, watching him, gaze up at the stunning sky and wondering to herself.

He didn't turn or say a thing. He wanted to wait and take it slow with this one, though he knew he was probably already in love with her, and if not just yet then certainly soon. Either way, he thought, he was bound to lose all of himself in no time. He had known that fact the instant he saw her.

Madison was the kind of girl every man yearned to call his own: respectable, beautiful and playful. And it didn't surprise him that he had seen all of those qualities in her almost instantly. But he had promised himself he would wait and let her come to him.

That way, she could warm up slowly to him and they could both digest the enormity of what they were already feeling for each other. He wanted this to be exactly the way she wanted it because he knew she did. He'd have to watch himself though. Something about this firecracker had him comfortably on edge.

She stood right behind him now, her tight grip on the back of the bench steadying her. Her lungs filled with his scent, making her head spin.

"Do you come here often?" Her voice was tiny and a little unsure and her mind was now racing.

What was she doing? Meeting a perfect stranger — a male stranger — in the middle of the night when she was supposed to be studying and engaged!

. . . a very male stranger who not only comforted her, but had managed to make her laugh on probably the worst night of her life. A stranger with very brown eyes, eyes that had the power to melt her troubles away. And rough, hardworking hands.

. . . a tall, handsome stranger who gave a spoiled, upset princess the shirt off his back. She almost turned to leave when she realized what she was doing but stopped herself. There was something else about this guy, beyond good manners and great arms that had her coming back for more. She was going to find out exactly what it was.

"You're late, princess," he answered in an easy tone, keeping his back to her.

"And you're trespassing."

"Really? Now that's an interesting accusation. How do you figure when I'm the genius that tends that very grass you're standing on?"

"I understand you are part of the grounds crew but I believe my bedroom balcony is not on your list of responsibilities." Her voice was calm and even. There was something about a good debate that always got her blood pumping.

"Actually, you're right. There is something up there, besides the hibiscus, that has caught my attention . . ."

"Oh yeah? And what would that be?" A little flirting never hurt either.

"You got a pretty sorry looking geranium up there too." His mouth spread into a smile. His back still faced her but he could feel the fury. Her silence confirmed it.

"You aren't use to being teased, are you?" he broke the silence finally.

"No, I'm not," she huffed. He had done it again and she couldn't figure out how.

"Come here and tell me why." The inches

of distance between them were driving him crazy.

"Well, I guess I was just never really in the position to be teased." She came around the side of the bench but continued until she reached the water's edge and then just stood, looking out into the pond. "I've been private schooled my whole life and social-izing meant tight shoes and guests twice my age. My best friend is sixty-eight."

"Sounds rough, princess. So you're so-cially challenged; explains a lot. But I for-give you. You're lucky; I'm a very forgiving guy."

She didn't answer. She looked a million miles away. He wondered where she was right now, what she was thinking or remem-bering. Her hands crossed over her chest and held her shoulders in tight fists. A shield, but what was she blocking out, hiding from, protecting herself against?

He came up behind her. He had to know if it was him she was guarding herself against. They had only shared one night together and though it had been the most magical night of his life, he wondered now if she hadn't felt anything at all or if she had al-ready made up her mind about him. Women like Madison hardly ever gave Johnny a first chance once they found out what he did and where he came from. Nonetheless, he already found himself ready to beg for a second with her. He certainly knew when he was asking for the stars but he wasn't ready to give up on her yet.

Johnny took two steps towards her back and slowly moved closer until she seemed relaxed enough for him to smooth his large hands over her delicate shoulders.

The charge from the contact was unmistakable but more importantly she didn't flinch and hadn't scared at his touch. They were both surprised and awed by the current that passed through them. She continued to stare out into the calm water, wishing she could be as still on the inside.

Spurred by her relaxed demeanor, he looked closer. Her skin was warm beneath his touch yet there were tiny bumps covering the white, porcelain skin of her bare shoulders. It was dark and the only thing illuminating them was the silver moonlight.

"Cold?" His voice was husky and just a whisper in her ear.

"No," Madison managed to answer. He was so close and his touch so gentle and warm she almost forgot to answer him with audible words. Such formalities seemed useless when they were communicating so much more without them.

Johnny trailed his hand up her neck and ran his fingers through her short, golden hair. Soft, he noted, and fragrant. He wrapped another hand below her elbows and around her middle. She hummed her pleasure in response to his exploring touch.

Slow, go slow with this one, he had to remind himself but something about the moonlight and the water had him going with his gut more than any kind of logic.

She had swayed gently in front of him and he feared she might go down like the night before. But it seemed almost like a different unsteadiness, like a floating or a drifting.

He moved in closer and felt her press against him in answer.

Johnny heard a waltz in his head and hummed it as he laid his cheek against her head. They swayed together now to the waltz he hummed and he turned her gently towards him. He wanted to look at her perfect face, to stare into her big eyes in the silvery moonlight and make sure he wasn't dreaming. She turned gracefully with his strong lead and, keeping her eyes closed, danced slowly in his arms.

When her face finally rose, he bent to answer it. Their lips met in a deep, warm union.

He felt it then, a small tremor of her flesh

beneath his hands. It was so faint and quick he almost missed it, but he didn't. He was all senses at the moment, touch, smell, sound, and her reaction had him wanting more, a quickened pulse, a deep, long shudder maybe or a moan. He wanted to feel her feeling something at his touch, a sign of the power he felt and hoped she did too. His hands closed over her shoulders firmly. Could she feel it now, under his strong grip? Would she almost miss it too, or would she simply pretend it wasn't there and act like it never happened?

He stopped then and Madison opened her dreamy eyes, raising them after the moment it took to clear them. He searched her face, her eyes, the utterly clear and endless blueness of them, for the answer to his fears, his longings. Was she actually accepting this poor, orphaned artist who worked for her father?

He could truly love her, a revelation that had initially scared him, though he didn't scare easy. He had heard of this girl, had thought about her ever since arriving and now, here she was, closer than he had ever let anyone get to him in a long time. He could want her for life and the thought gave his own tough skin a shiver, but the fantasy of a lifetime paled against the thought of the right now, the present moment. What he wanted now was to take her and give her so much in return. He could feel every want in her body and knew he could satisfy them all. He wanted to show her what his touch could do and the pleasures he could give her. The air hung all around, blurry and dizzy. The lilacs' thick fragrance surrounded them.

Funny, he hadn't remembered the crew planting any lilac bushes . . .

"What? Why are you looking at me that way?" Startled now, Madison quickly snapped out of her dreamy state and a little shake of her head had her feet back on the ground.

"Just admiring the view," Johnny managed, snapping out of something quite powerful himself. Charm had always been his key, unlocking many doors and hearts. He had always used the few tools he had to survive this world.

Her eyes narrowed on his and he could feel her slipping away.

"Honestly, it's nothing. Come here." He pulled her into the curve of his chest and wrapped his arms around her. "Got the other night out of your system? You were pretty bummed. Want to talk about it?" he asked to distract her.

He wasn't quite ready to tell her what was really running through his mind or to profess his love. Once again, he had to remind himself to go slow and let her lead the way.

The other night, the party! Madison wanted to jump out of his arms at the mention of it but the memory failed to have its usual effects. She had been brought back to it many times in the past two days and its mention was always accompanied by a wave of sickness, large and overwhelming. But just now, safe in Johnny's arms, she felt nothing. Well, not nothing. What she was feeling now was good, unexplainable, but very, very good. In fact, Madison couldn't remember the last time she had felt so calm in her own skin or so relaxed with another person.

"No," she answered.

Smiling and completely relieved, Madison decided she wouldn't tell Johnny the details of the party, though she knew he had a right to know. She couldn't, not yet at least and not while she was having so much fun. She had never been this reckless in her life and was enjoying every forbidden moment.

"Okay, fine, I get it. It's your party." Johnny shrugged it off. He knew something had happened. After all, he had witnessed the effects of that something, hadn't he? But he also knew that she'd come around soon enough; he didn't need to push just yet. Instead, he wrapped her up again in his arms and nearly took her off her feet, an action which delighted her to no end. She was completely amazed by his size and strength and he was equally amused by her delicate frame and near weightlessness.

"Now, how did you know it was a celebration in my honor?" She broke away then and took his hand to show him her favorite spot to sit and wet her feet in the pond.

"What? Oh, no, that's just my motto. You know, life is like a party — your party." Johnny caught the confusion in her face and decided he had better explain. "It's like you are the host and you have to decide all the important stuff to make it work."

They both sat on a slate of rock and Madison removed her sandals. The sensual arch of her small foot had him struggling to keep his train of thought.

"Go on," she encouraged him, not sure of where he was going yet.

"Okay, so you get to choose the food and who you'll invite and the music and games. It's really just a metaphor for life.

"But mostly I like it because life should be fun in the end. And everything you do and choose determines how it'll go and how much fun you'll have. Life should be your party. Make any sense?"

"Yes actually, it does. I like it," she decided and rested her chin on her knee.

"What's wrong?"

"I just wasn't raised with that prerogative. I was taught differently, a fact that has become a lot more evident to me over the past two days." Her father's smiling face flashed before her eyes as his mouth spoke the most unanticipated words . . .

Johnny's eyes narrowed, now it was her turn to explain. "I've been taught to do as I'm told. Decisions are, for the most part, made for me, the important ones anyways, because of who I am, who my family is and the implications of the Carlton name and reputation."

She looked at him with sad eyes, now thinking about how different they really were. He was spouting life lessons on important decisions and fun and she wasn't even allowed to decide who she would marry and spend the rest of her life with. It was all so very sad but she couldn't let herself think of that now. Right now, there was only the magical sky and Johnny.

"You don't really believe that though. I know you don't." She only nodded her head in response, silently willing the warmth of a few moments ago to stay just a while longer.

"You're different," he said but she only shook her head. "You can be different if you want to be. Madison, hey, look at me." He grabbed both her shoulders now, forcing her eyes on his. Could this be what had upset her the first night they met? She wouldn't answer him, couldn't even look at him. It was too late; he had realized it too. They were from separate worlds.

"Don't you tell me you believe that bullshit? This is your life, the one and only. Don't lie and tell me you're one of them." He almost sneered the last words, one of them, as though it were the most awful thing in the world to be anything like her family or the elite community of billionaires they belonged to.

"I'm a Carlton, Johnny." She slipped on her shoes and slowly got to her feet.

"Not that! I know your name, your ancestors, your reputation. That's not what I mean and that isn't what makes you. Your heart and your courage, your intellect and wit, they are what make you who you really are. Your decisions and goals are what should determine what you'll do in this world, in this precious life, not them. You are not just a name."

He was worked up now and had to try to

calm down, but he had to get through to her too. "Tell me you don't believe all that stuff about family money and class status." He had feared that he could never live up to her name but not nearly as much as he had feared not ever living up to her as a person, that was far worse to imagine. The money was so superficial, though, and he could hardly believe someone as smart and down-to-earth as Madison would give in to it all and allow it to shadow any real relationship she might have with someone.

"You're wrong, Johnny. I am their creation. I am who they have made me and I will never forget that. I am the only heir to the Carlton fortune! Don't you understand what that means?" But how could he? And how could he not have known that her lineage would always be the dark cloud hanging over their heads? He only stared back with an ominously blank stare.

"Oh Johnny, it doesn't matter. I intend to fulfill my role as such. That's all that matters. They may hold my life in their hands but only because I owe them that much. Your life may be a party — your party — but some are not at liberty to make the same claim on theirs. I'm sorry we are so different. And I wish you wouldn't look at me like that."

She had to hold back the tears that burned her eyes. She wouldn't let him see her falter a second time. She didn't need to be rescued this time. She believed what she was saying to him. The past couple of days had been awesome because of him. In that short span of time, he had taught her things about herself that she had never known before. What was happening between them, however, was purely physical, she assured herself; it was not real. It couldn't be. Her real life was behind the terrace and mansion walls.

She would respect her family and defend its honor and traditions, but the sheer disappointment in his eyes as he looked at her was unmistakable. It pulled violently at her aching heart. If she was doing the right thing then why did she feel so sore and exposed?

He had no more respect for her. She could feel it. His arms had dropped and he had stepped back, appalled at her response. The foot between them felt like a hundred miles and her sadness only deepened. Still, she held her position and waited for his response. She deserved that much from him at least.

His eyes finally left her face. He had lost her. She wasn't one of them. He knew she wasn't. If she was, what transpired between them never could have. It didn't matter though. What mattered was she wanted to play by their rules.

She had made every one of his darkest fears real and it now created a wedge between them that was so wide, neither could reach out to the other.

The anger drained from him, leaving only sadness. He had been wrong about her and knew when to admit it. It was time to cut his losses. He was used to doing that but this time he figured he had lost big. She was loyal to daddy at least. He had to give her that. He just wasn't important enough to her, and it was his own fault for expecting to be in the first place. Sad, he would have slain dragons for this princess.

He watched her standing there. The bravest face he had ever seen her wear was doing a damn shit job of hiding the horror in her eyes. He could see that she knew this was good-bye, so that was all that was left to give her.

"Well then, it was nice knowing you, Miss Madison Carlton. I believe my time is up and I apologize for consuming two days of your predestined life. You better return to your throne and I'll return to mine."

He wasn't going to make this part easy on her either. If she wanted to be Madison

Carlton and carry all the burdens that name implied then she'd better start realizing what her decision would cost her.

"Don't you dare start with that sarcastic attitude when I've just been completely honest with you about my situation." Rage clouded her clear, blue eyes, turning them the color and consistency of ice. How dare he treat her like a stranger when they had both clearly become more than that in the past days?

"So that's what you call it? Honesty? Haven't seen this kind of honesty since the first night I found you running and screaming from that castle you call home. You started with the sarcasm; I'm just finishing with it, princess."

He turned and left her there, standing by the edge of the pond. The water stood as still as death behind her. He was both sad and disappointed in her and for them yet he was proud of himself.

Johnny found his favorite spot a couple yards up, where he could think and brood. And as he did, thoughts of his own father suddenly surfaced without warning, but the memories were surprisingly comforting this time. Johnny knew his father would have been proud of him for sticking to what he believed in and what was right. But it was the only thing Johnny could do when it came to Madison Carlton.

He could be strong enough for the both of them, he knew that, but that wasn't what he wanted. Going up against Julian Carlton would take more strength than ten men. It would take the strength of one special woman.

Madison had made her decision and Johnny would respect that. He'd even try to get over her, over and above. He'd do his job and live his life the only way he knew how, exactly how he wanted. He'd be the best of the crew and, come fall, he'd be the one deciding if he'd return the following season to work for the Carltons or not.

Johnny knew that once he poured his heart and soul into these acres they would be crawling with every newspaper and artsy magazine on the planet. And Johnny would get the credit he deserved; they all would. He'd be in high demand all over the world and once the money started rolling in, he could concentrate on his true love: painting.

He'd be something one day and then they'd all see that you don't always have to follow everyone else's rules.

Chapter Thirteen

"You must hurry, Madison. The Leemons will be here shortly and your mamma will not be pleased when you're still dressing and not greeting."

Elizabeth bustled about the Victorian-styled room with purpose. The place was unusually messy and it looked like Madison had evacuated nearly her entire wardrobe in search of an outfit for the afternoon.

"Oh, Elizabeth. I don't know what to wear. I just can't seem to put anything together that might be suitable."

Madison emerged from her bathroom draped in a bright red and yellow Kimono. A smiling dragon breathed fire and wound its strong body across the thick silk. Traveling had garnered her an extensive as well as interesting collection of ethnic items but the dragon Kimono was by far her favorite and recently she seemed to live in it. Without her usual energy she was happy to remain wrapped in it forever and was hesitant to even remove it for the day's meeting.

"Ah, you will be wonderful in anything. I'm sure you can find a simple pantsuit. The pastel peach with a white scarf, perhaps? Something light and simple, to brighten your mood.

"You are so good at putting yourself together and I don't believe there is not a thing to wear in this heap. Come on now, get yourself dressed. You can't stay in that housecoat forever," Elizabeth warned and Madison had to bite her tongue from challenging her on it. She was in no mood for guests, much less her fiancé and future in-laws. Madison almost burst out in tears again at the mere thought. She had always envisioned herself grooming for hours and as happy as a butterfly when her fiancé was due for lunch.

It was a sad situation and she still wasn't sure what she was going to do about it all. Should she admit her reservations and let her family help her with the transition or act as thrilled as a bride-to-be should be and save her parents from the embarrassment of having an ungrateful daughter?

Elizabeth gave up righting the place and searched through a pile of garments for the outfit she had dreamed up for the day. She had to get Madison down to the greeting room before Julian and Victoria arrived there first.

Madison wandered as she thought and arrived at the glassed doors of her balcony. She didn't step out into the day, however. She simply laid a hand on the sheer fabric that floated in the breeze and looked out into the gardens.

Was he out there today, working nearby?

"Start with this camisole," Elizabeth said as she continued to rummage.

Could he see her bedroom window or the mansion at all from where he was this very minute? She swept a dreamy hand through her messy hair as she pondered.

"Madison, you'll use the beige flats and crystal clasp. Did you hear me, child?"

Would he think of her today as she had thought of him every day since they met? A deep sigh escaped her pale, parted lips.

"Madison!"

Madison startled to attention and regarded her old friend with wide eyes, as if seeing her for the first time. Elizabeth stood clutching the peach jacket and pants in one arm and beige flats in the other. Silver strands had escaped her low bun and her round face shimmered with perspiration. With pursed lips and concerned eyes, Elizabeth heaved the items from her arms onto the large bed, let out an exasperated sigh and sat.

"What is going on here?"

"Nothing. I'm fine, I swear," Madison said unconvincingly as tears began to well up.

"Let us hear it" was all Elizabeth said before Madison threw herself down beside her and began.

"Oh, I just don't know what's wrong with me. Oh, of course I do. Did you love Joseph when you married him?"

"Ah, this was very long ago." Elizabeth shook her head and wondered how she could possibly help. Madison's life was so different than the one she had led. How could she guide her now or speak about such things as love and life when those days were so different than the days Madison was up against?

"You must remember, please. I need to know." Madison's whole body pleaded and her face was a kaleidoscope of emotion. She saw desperation, confusion and unrest in the young woman and somehow Elizabeth knew that emotions didn't age. "Okay, Madison. What do you want to know?"

"Did you marry for love?"

"People marry for many reasons, Madison. For money or debt, for family or convenience. Each has a story to tell and, I suspect, one that may be quite fantastic compared with mine. Scandal and all that, but my story is very simple. I indeed married for love."

"Tell me about it," Madison said solemnly and took a seat in front of her old friend. She watched and listened to Elizabeth's story for the answers she knew she'd find. She was completely ready for the impact they would have on the rest of her life.

"Elizabeth, where is my daughter?"

"Ah, Miss Victoria, it is unlike Madison to be tardy, but you may allow her a few more moments as she is very nervous about this afternoon."

"Yes, of course, Elizabeth," Julian chimed in. "She probably wants to look her best for Arthur. Such a good girl, always trying to please."

Julian milled about the large guest room, fussing with this and that as he smiled tensely at Victoria. She, on the other hand, was the picture of calm, sitting completely still, hands folded in lap, waiting patiently. Her dark, wild curls were pulled loosely into an elegant French braid and the bright sundress and wide-brimmed hat she sported mirrored her relaxed mood. She was a constant contrast to her nervous husband.

Elizabeth set the tray of refreshments

down on the antique coffee table and returned to the kitchen to continue preparing for lunch. She knew the afternoon would be pleasurable for both families yet she also knew it would be less fruitful than they had planned for both their firstborns.

Madison had spoken of love and listened to the story that was Elizabeth's life with serious and passionate eyes. Yet somehow Elizabeth knew that her young charge didn't have the young Arthur in mind and it didn't worry her one bit. Madison was a good girl, raised into a wonderful woman by her own hand. She was certain Madison would do the right thing, no matter what she decided in this lifetime.

"Too much pressure on the poor thing" was all she murmured upon her exit.

"What was that?" Joseph was also in the kitchen, assisting his wife with the heavier serving trays.

"Ah, it's Madison. It's all the pressure they put on her. I don't like it."

"Yes, but do you not remember the pressure we were under as youngsters?" He smiled in remembrance. "And we survived it just fine." He took her hand in his and rubbed his thumb over the only ring on her fingers. The plain gold band warmed at his touch.

"Not without a fight, if I remember right," she agreed.

"Well, when you fight for love it's always worth it." He lifted a wide silver tray and smiled.

"Yes, I suppose that is what I told her too."

"Told who?"

"Never mind that, Joseph. Come back for the lemonade pitcher when you're done with that platter."

Chapter Fourteen

"Johnny baby, Kay says you better get out to the west-end gazebo pronto." Al knocked once before entering Johnny's small cabin. She was a tall woman with fiery red curls and dark green eyes. A pale yellow tank top, khaki shorts and work boots were the few items covering her brown, freckled skin.

Al had been part of the Carlton grounds crew three years in a row and the only worker to last past the first. Despite being the sole female worker, she was pulling pretty high rank among them.

She found Johnny spread out comfortably on his bed, filthy from the morning's work and scribbling on one of his pads. His long, quick fingers were black from the dark lead of his tools and his shaggy, sun-kissed strands hung in his eyes as his head bowed into his work. She breathed in his musky scent, sweat and the outdoors, and watched his talented hands at work.

Al remembered back, way back, to when those strong hands used to touch her, rough and calloused. When she used to drag her nails across his hard chest to let him know she needed his hands on her. Now, she never missed the chance to let him know how great they had been together.

She had been absolutely thrilled when she caught the news that Johnny Sparks had won a spot on the Carlton team. Not only because it was a great opportunity for him to get his hands dirty again but because it meant they'd be working together all summer. And he really did look better than ever.

Johnny barely looked up when Al barged in.

"Ahh, he's probably looking for the supplies that came over today. Would you just tell him I stocked the south tower with the shade seed? That's what he's probably looking for. That's where we're going to be needing it the most. Pond's perimeter is completely covered 'cause of those willows. Massive suckers, aren't they, Al? Beautiful, but massive. That seed will really help with the bald spots."

He spoke to her absentmindedly, as he would a close friend, a buddy or a sister. It didn't hurt so much as piss her off. Al wasn't hurt easy. In fact, it was he who had been hurt when Al took off one winter for a contract job in L.A., leaving Johnny with a dying father and a ten-year-old father-son landscaping biz gone belly up. Rough times, but Johnny pulled through. Buried his father and Sparks Landscaping in one afternoon then headed north to start a new life.

"No, baby, it isn't that. He said it was important." She surveyed his room, his endless stashes of paper and charcoals. It had been a while since she visited his cabin. Maybe two months, she thought as she counted back to the season's start. She remembered the first night he had arrived at the mansion, particularly the special reuniting she had planned for the two of them. A secret late-night reunion for old times' sake. She hadn't gotten a chance to see much of his room then, though she'd gotten her fill of something else that night.

She had planned it all so perfectly, making it so he couldn't resist her. The part she hadn't planned on was all those old feelings resurfacing. Hell, she hated to admit it, but she was still in love with him. She was four years from thirty and still mad over her high school crush. It was so typical and Al just hated typical.

"What kind of important?" Now he looked up, almost interested in what she had to say. He had worked long and hard all morning for this break, though to Johnny a break meant getting back to work on his portfolio.

"Well, it might have something to do with that blonde that's been hanging around the main storehouse."

She saw the startled look come over his perfect face.

"Kay thought it was a Carlton come to complain about a tree or bush but apparently the only thing she was troubling about was you. He said she wanted to know your domain and cabin number."

He didn't respond. He didn't have to. She could tell he knew exactly what she was talking about. And knowing he wasn't going to spill it, especially to her, she took a seat on the small bed beside his crossed legs.

"Look, he doesn't want you causing any problems around here. We all know what a great contract this is and he doesn't want to lose you or his own job." She was partly concerned but mostly not. "I thought you preferred redheads to blondes anyways."

Her wide mouth spread into a grin as she reached under his dusty T-shirt. She'd take his mind off that blonde for him, for the both of them.

She closed her eyes and dragged her nails across his firm belly, feeling the need rising between her thighs. She quickly felt the recklessness of their youth come over her, swamping her mind with wet, fluid thoughts as she swam in the pleasure of her senses. The smell of him and the heat that radiated from his body had her own softening against his and her mind losing all control.

With distant eyes, Johnny pulled away and headed for the shower, leaving Al alone on the bed and as worked up as ever.

He had a lot to chew on given this new piece of information. Could the blonde Al was talking about be Madison? He had wondered about her every day since they had agreed to disagree, but he never thought he would hear from her again. The pain was too real. As much for him as it was for her, he was certain.

He pulled off his work clothes and ran some hot water in the shower.

"Johnny baby, if you're not going to join me over here on the bed then I'm going to have to take care of this myself," Al threatened through the cabin's thin bathroom door.

"Do what you got to do, beautiful. I have complete faith in you," he called back without doubt and turned the water to cold. He had to admit, that redhead could still get him going.

Chapter Fifteen

Earlier that day, Madison sat directly across from Arthur Leemon at their own private table on the mansion's terrace. Their parents were nearby but out of earshot so that the only voices heard were those raised in laughter. They had purposely been given privacy and time to get further acquainted as their parents worked out the details of the merger.

The day was quickly growing humid. The large canvas umbrella they sat under offered Madison shade from the blazing sun but not from the rising heat. And the sun seemed to follow Arthur ruthlessly, making his upper lip and brow shiny with perspiration. His already small eyes squinted against its strong glare.

She watched him grin at her, oblivious to the pools of sweat collecting around his neck, as though even he could not believe his good luck. To him, Madison really was just another prize he had won or, in this case, a present he was simply given.

Without much to say to each other, they sipped Elizabeth's famous lemonade and enjoyed the view of the gardens from the terrace. The fresh lemon pulp that clung to the walls of their glasses looked like snow-flakes and reminded Madison to enjoy the good weather while it was still around.

Though she had lived in the mansion her entire life, Madison was stilled awed by the sight that lay before her. Yet even it could not placate her tensing muscles and bunching fists that morning. With each passing moment her frustration grew. It angered her completely when she thought about the arrangement her parents were construing that very minute with the Leemons.

She hadn't thought of it before but now she realized the extent of what they were doing. Arthur would be given all of this simply because he would marry into it, because it was an appropriate and sound merger between the wealthiest and oldest families in Southampton.

Madison bitterly tried to justify her parents' decision and actions. She couldn't believe they were doing this just to spite her contemporary and free spirit. It had to be more, much more.

She knew that roots were essential to the

beginnings of great families, that establishing a name and a history meant creating century-old traditions and honoring them. Money, she thought, ensured that a family remained prosperous and respected by the generations that followed. Her parents knew that too, a little too well. And because they had had a daughter, they felt they had to work harder to preserve both their status and their name for future generations. It was what their parents had done for them and what her parents were to do for her.

They were going to marry her off to equal wealth in order to continue the cycle their ancestors had sweated to create. And they were going to do it before she got her wings and flew right out of synch with what they were planning for her.

Would she fit nicely into place and accept her role as her mother and grandmother had before her? Would she bring babies into this family and one day place them appropriately, as if they were just a role to be filled, a part to be played, a tool to be used in the tug-o-war that was power and money?

She felt helpless no longer. She had come to a realization since her talk with Elizabeth and though it meant taking a great risk, she wasn't afraid.

She looked over at Arthur, with his

straight back and handsome face, and she thought he looked delicate and manicured. She thought he looked ridiculous.

Madison instantly knew what she had to do if she didn't want to lose herself in this faceless game. She had denied herself the best thing that had ever happened to her and for what? For a family that could only see dollar signs, that's what. Madison knew that if she could be strong and sure in herself then she could show her parents how differently she wanted everything. She felt certain she could convince them how different it needed to be for her to be truly happy.

Chapter Sixteen

Johnny lay on his side and stared out at the large golden moon that hung in his window. It was the middle of the summer and past 2:00 A.M. and sleep was not going to come easily, as it hadn't for weeks now. Night after night he lay restless in his dark cabin, overcome with thought. His mind raced constantly, refusing to rest, unable to concentrate on either his art or his work.

He thought about life, past and future, and his father and his painting but mostly he thought of Madison and the short time they had shared together. Was she really trying to get in contact with him? If she was, he knew he couldn't meet her. For her sake and his own he would stay away from her. If it really was as she had described it then there was no hope and no point in exploring what they could never have.

The soft thud that emanated from just outside his window was hardly anything of interest to him until it came again. With strained ears, Johnny decided it sounded more like a struggle than any of the small rodents he had grown accustomed to sharing his cabin with.

The soft noises continued until Johnny saw a small crown of gold bobbing in his window. A smile came over his face and he wanted to laugh out loud with delight, yet he remained perfectly still in his bed, watching his princess scale his one-story castle.

Madison struggled to find her footing against the smooth logs of the wall. Her tiny arms barely held the weight of her body as she reached for the window's small sill. The single glass was a crack open as she knew it would be.

He watched as she finally pushed the window farther open and slipped easily through the small space. He was careful to keep his grinning face out of the moonlight and his breath even enough to sound as though he were sound asleep.

She finally managed to find her footing as her eyes adjusted to the small, moonlit room. Pleased with herself, she stood over Johnny's sleeping body, both hands on hips.

She breathed in deeply and was amazed when nerves didn't turn her stomach. She was sure she'd be a wreck and thought she might not be able to pull it off. She had her father's nerves when it came to things like this.

A break-in was hardly her style and a break-in for the purpose of seducing the sleeping victim was completely unlike her. The sudden change in her behavior didn't concern her but excited her instead. She realized she hadn't really been herself ever since she had met Johnny Sparks this revealing summer and she liked that revelation, deep down to the depths she was still discovering existed within her.

She breathed in deeper and savored the scent that wafted all around her. It had been one agonizing month since they had last spoken and Madison was determined to reconnect with the only man she had ever felt completely comfortable and herself with. He had been right about her: she *was* different.

Madison wanted to make up for the time they had lost and thought this would be the perfect way to get him remembering her again. Only now that she had executed her plan, she didn't have the heart to wake him or the nerve to face him just yet. She had mapped out the break-in perfectly but was less prepared for what she was actually going to say to him once she was inside.

She took a minute to think and caught

herself looking around at the personal items littering the room. It was messy and the possessions were few but the room was Johnny. She lifted a thick drawing pad to the soft moonlight and studied the images in it. The sketches were detailed and beautiful and the subject was her. She was taken aback by the detail of his work. He had captured her features so accurately that the sketch could have passed as a photograph; her mouth was plump and dark with youth and her eyes sparkled with innocence. Her hair danced around her ears and chin and her neckline and shoulders were delicately carved and shaded. Once Madison recovered from the awkwardness of it, she was touched and so proud of the talent that had brought a few lines of charcoal to life.

She was also feeling a little guilty snooping around his room but she couldn't help herself. She had never been here before, hadn't even known which cabin was his until she got up the nerve to do some investigating. What a kick! She was starting to feel like a regular private investigator and it was exhilarating.

Madison knew she was a dreamer. Her wild imagination often took her to other times and places she secretly yearned for but this time she had decided to make her dream a reality. This time her desire was so strong, so important, that she had to at least try to make it happen. It was all up to her, if she could just be strong. Johnny had shown her that she could.

Her free hand reached for the desk drawer. Within its nooks and crannies, she hoped she'd find more clues about the stranger she thought she could love.

"Nothing here worth stealing; you're better off taking me instead."

A short yelp escaped Madison's lips as she startled at the low voice in the darkness of the room. The heavy pad slipped from her grasp and hit the floor. The portraits scattered and her striking face decorated the nearly empty floor.

"I thought you were asleep." She spoke to a shadow at the head of his narrow bed.

"And what exactly were you going to do with me while I slept?" he asked comically though he really did want to know what she had planned for him.

"I was going to seduce you." She dragged a hand through her hair and let out an annoyed huff before the embarrassment of what she had just blurted out hit her.

"Not with all that racket you weren't." He was thoroughly amused now.

"Well, it's my first break-and-enter and I

thought I did very well." She crossed her arms over her chest stubbornly and he was glad to have her back.

He reached an arm out to her and drew her into the shadows with him. The faint scent of her body, baby powder and lilacs, drove him wild.

He could hear her breath catch when he took her now trembling hands in his. He rubbed them firmly to soothe and warm them and then brought them to his chest so she could feel the pounding of his own heart.

"Have you thought of me?" she asked the darkness.

"Every second," he replied honestly and caught her sobbing face in his hands.

They were both overcome with emotion the minute their hands met in the darkness and all they could do was hold each other in a long, rocking hug.

Yes, she had felt the magic between them too.

Al was just finishing up her last repetition of push-ups when she heard light footsteps between the crew cabins. It was so quiet out here that she usually heard the mice playing in the grass, so she was very interested when it was sounds of human life she detected.

Bedtime came early for the guys. They worked hard and slept even harder, so she knew it couldn't be staff. She was usually the only one up at these hours, working out in the cool night air and moonlight. It was the only time she could get some privacy from the guys. Her ritual not only soothed her muscles after a long day on the job but also did something magical for her soul.

Al loved her work at the mansion but it was physically challenging, even for some of the guys, so she worked her body hard to ensure she never had to ask for a hand. They looked for any excuse to remind her that she was female, and she wasn't about to go giving them any more.

She judged, by the direction of the sound, that someone was walking from the main house and heading south. Not much there she thought, just two more cabins then you hit nothing but forest. Ah huh, cabin twelve was Johnny's. She should have guessed it.

She had suspected he had acquired an admirer, maybe even a crush, about a month ago but she was sure that that was ancient history.

Al had to strain her ears against the night's sounds but soon it all became crystal clear. Snooping around the main storehouse . . . pinching info out of Kay and now a late night interlude. It was all so romantic. Al had to keep from gagging.

She had known Johnny was involved with the Carlton daughter a few weeks back and just as she suspected, it hadn't lasted long. She had even warned him against the idea when he had first arrived. Al knew Johnny must have been suckered; the old man's daughter was blonde and cuter than pie. What man wouldn't at least try? She could hardly blame them. Princess Blondie got to defy dear old daddy and Johnny got to be the one she used for the job. It was all so convenient.

She peered over at Johnny's cabin and watched the skinny, rich kid struggle to climb into the already open window. Pathetic, she thought, and had to stop herself from imagining little-miss-perfect falling and cracking an ankle.

She'd let the girl have her fun with Johnny for now because when the time was right she would have him back and all to herself. She had let him go once but she wasn't going to let him get away a second time.

Chapter Seventeen

"Victoria? You may see him now."

Elizabeth held Victoria's shaky shoulder and led her into the dimly lit sick room.

Red-rimmed eyes stared down at Julian's still body. "Is he comfortable?" was all she could manage from her raw throat.

"Yes, my dear. He's in no pain." The old doctor gathered his tools quietly. His steady hands carefully placed each of them into a black leather case. He wanted to give Victoria privacy now that he had done all he could do for his patient. When he was done, he took her into his arms and held her weak body there firmly.

"We're okay, Victoria, just a little scare this time 'round. Be strong for him; he needs you the most through all of this. I can only ease his body through it, but you, you've got the most important job. You will ease his soul." Victoria let out a soft sob and he released her into the arms of Elizabeth.

"Good night. I will see you all in the

morning." And with that, the old doctor left the room and met Joseph in the hallway.

"I'll see ya out, Doc, and thanks for coming so quick." Joseph shook the doctor's hand and then led him to one of the side entrances.

"The stroke was very mild, Joseph. We were lucky this time. Next time we might not be so fortunate. Do you understand what I'm saying? You know we are at the end now. With this kind of blood disease his organs will continue to fail . . . It won't be much longer."

Joseph bowed his head and nodded in understanding.

"He's out for the night now. I want you to call me if he wakes. We'll run some tests to determine the extent of the damage at this point. I believe it will be very little, hardly detectable. Keep your eye on Victoria, man. She'll need some looking after as well. Good night."

Johnny was walking Madison home early that morning when they both saw the car pulling away. Madison stopped dead in her tracks, all color draining from her face. They had continued to meet each other only at night and in secret, to chat or to sleep in the gardens or in his cabin, and upon sunrise he would regretfully walk her home. At this rate he was averaging about two hours of sleep per night but had never felt more invigorated in his life.

"Who could that be at this time?" Johnny asked casually.

"That's our private doctor." Her voice was small and weak in answer.

"Doc —" Johnny began but Madison had already taken off towards the mansion, sprinting the rest of the way.

Johnny quickly followed after her, and they both slid into the dark house. He stayed close behind as she tore down hallway after hallway. He felt the majesty of the place the minute his old runners met the marble floor of the mansion. He had never been inside the main house before.

"Elizabeth?" Madison called out into the dark hall but only her own voice echoed back to them in a chilling mimic. The ominous house was as quiet and as dark as a tomb until Elizabeth emerged from a soft glowing room. She caught Madison's wild wrists in her hands and pulled her close. Johnny stopped too, careful to remain in the shadow of a doorway, and watched.

The embrace pulled at his heart. He saw the older woman wrap a thick arm around Madison's tiny waist as she gently petted her head in the silver light of the hallway. She whispered cooing sounds into Madison's ear as she slowly explained what had happened.

"Your papa, Madison —" was all he could hear clearly and Johnny knew the rest wouldn't be good news. He instantly wished he was the one holding Madison, rocking her in his arms.

Madison fell to her knees then, racked with grief. He could feel the old love these women shared as well as their new sorrow. An older man emerged from a hallway then and murmured something to the older woman. She nodded gravely as he folded Madison's limp, sobbing body into his arms. They carried her away, Madison obviously not wanting to see what was in that softly lit room, and Johnny wanted to leave the hallway too. This was what family meant and he wanted them to have every moment of it. He understood the need for family, privacy and sorrow. It was universal. And he knew what it meant to lose a father, to illness or to death.

As he quietly slipped out of the mansion the same way he had come just moments before, bounding after Madison, he envisioned what the next couple of days and weeks would hold for her. He also envisioned himself there with her, every step of the way. It would be rough, on both of them, but he wasn't about to let her go through it alone. If he had it his way, she'd never have to go through anything by herself again.

Chapter Eighteen

"Julian? Dear sweet Julian . . . I'm so sorry. It wasn't supposed to be this way . . . We were supposed to grow old and ugly together." Victoria pressed her wet cheek to his when she was finally alone with her husband.

Her limbs trembled violently and she felt like she was trudging through mud. She finally understood that this was it. Julian might recover this time but it was the beginning of the end and everyone, except him, knew it. She had been in denial for so long that the horrific reality of his condition now came as a tremendous shock to her mind and body. She suddenly didn't care anymore about the carefully guarded secrets she had kept for years or the merger. Now there was only Julian and the unbearable tearing of her heart as she watched her husband's suffering and slow death.

"Don't leave me . . . if you can hear me, darling . . . please stay here with me . . . just a little longer. I need you so much. I don't know if I can keep this family together without you . . . I just don't know what is going to become of me. Please, Julian, open your eyes. Can you hear me? Don't go, please, God. I love you too much."

She had tried just sitting and watching him as he slipped in and out of consciousness but found she only jumped at every labored breath he drew. Pacing had only made her dizzy and more confused, so now she lay beside him, pressing her face to his and cooing to calm herself and him, though she was almost certain he couldn't hear her. Both the pain and the medication kept him unconscious most of the time which, at this point, proved to be a merciful blessing.

"I love you. You are everything . . . please don't leave me. Come back to me, darling. What will I do here without my sweet Julian?"

"I . . . love . . . you . . . Victoria," he whispered hoarsely. It was the first time he had responded since the doctor had left and Victoria feared the painkillers might be wearing off. Without the doctor, however, she was powerless to help him.

"Julian? Oh Julian, please, no. Don't try to speak. I'm right here. I'm so sorry. I can't do anything more for you —" She collapsed into sobs again and Julian tried to reach out to comfort her but his arms were as heavy as lead. He had to take a moment to summon his strength again, and sheer determination gave him his breath back.

"Don't . . . cry. Sweet Victoria . . . everything will be . . . just fine. Please don't . . . be sad. I am sorry . . . I can't . . . be strong . . . for you now. I'm just . . . so tired . . ."

"Shhh, sweet Julian, sleep now. I'll be right here beside you. You're so brave. Rest now, please. I promise I won't cry anymore. Let's just lie here and be brave together. You're going to be alright, just fine. Now don't worry. Sleep."

She laced her fingers through his and buried her face in his shoulder. When she felt him slip away again, she surrendered to the grief in a long, chilling howl as her body heaved and shuddered, expelling the pain and sorrow from her core.

After a few moments, Joseph and Elizabeth appeared in the doorway, their eyes reflecting sadness and concern for both Julian and Victoria. They made a heart-wrenching sight, he stone-gray and almost lifeless and she clinging to his still body like a terrified child, and Elizabeth had to struggle to keep herself together. It was early morning and they had finally calmed Madison enough to leave her sleeping fitfully in her bed.

"She'll make herself sick if we let her carry on like this," Elizabeth said finally.

Joseph managed to pry Victoria's body from the bed and Elizabeth forced a sedative down her throat as she fought them with the little strength she had left.

"Don't touch me! I won't leave him. He needs me."

"You can stay right here with him," Joseph assured her, seating her in an armchair beside Julian's bedside. He unfolded a blanket from the closet to lay over her. She sat, curled up, hugging herself and rocking back and forth. Her eyes never left her husband's face, a deathly paleness sheathing her skin and dark bruises forming under her eyes.

"How do we know he is comfortable?" Victoria worried and asked Elizabeth again.

"The doctor said he should be out until noon. He'll be back before then. Try to get some sleep now. It's been a long night. You'll be no good to him if you make yourself sick."

Victoria shook her head but the powerful sedative was already working and she had to fight to keep her heavy eyes open.

"I don't want to miss him," she finally whispered to Elizabeth a moment before her eyes closed and refused to reopen.

"You won't. I'll wake you if anything

changes," Elizabeth promised and pulled the blanket up over Victoria's shoulders.

It was her turn to say a prayer for her little Julian. The happy child with dancing blue eyes and endless smiles flashed before her and she had to bow her head into her hands and weep silently for that dear, sweet boy.

Chapter Nineteen

Madison gathered her father in her arms as the noon sun filtered through the slightly parted curtains of the stuffy sick room.

When Elizabeth had first told her what had happened, she hadn't wanted to see him right away. She decided she'd see him in a couple hours, when the sun was up and when they would both be more like themselves. It may have been fear or denial but Madison just could not imagine what the strongest man she had ever known would look like in a sickbed. Now she knew and it was horrible.

When Madison had first entered the room she thought her father looked gray and lifeless but she held back the tears that threatened to spill and didn't say a word. She had shed enough tears for one morning. She simply held as much of him as her arms could hold and pressed her lips to his warm forehead.

She wanted him to wake up, just jump up like he did every morning, but she knew that wasn't going to happen. She also knew he wasn't going to ask for the morning paper, but she had brought it in anyway. Just feeling his slow heartbeat against hers was enough to put her mind at ease. She silently slid onto the bed beside him and hung on.

As the sun rose higher in the blue sky, Julian roused slightly and his blue eyes opened to an unusual day. Madison stirred too as he looked around curiously.

"I haven't found you curled at my side since you were five years old, angel," he whispered as Madison yawned and rubbed her sore eyes.

"Oh, Daddy, you scared me." Her face was concerned and he could see she had been crying. She hugged him hard, glad to hear his soothing voice.

It came back to him now. The numbness in his arm and an enormous pain he'd never felt before.

"I'm alright, just a little test of the will, that's all. And you know mine's stronger than anyone's." He spoke to calm her as much as he did to calm himself. He tried and found he couldn't move without extreme effort of his muscles and he suddenly realized that he was scared too.

Madison smiled at his unbelievable answer. Now she truly saw the strongest man she had ever known. Though she detected a slight slur when he spoke to her, she knew he was all there. He would bounce back in no time and was growing stronger by the moment.

Relieved at his state, Madison got herself up and began making the day for her father. Julian, utterly spent, simply laid his head back and watched her.

"So, I guess we will be needing this after all!" She held up the daily paper and beamed. His usual booming laughter came out as a low chuckle and he closed his eyes at the strain of it.

Madison settled into the chair that sat beside his bed, the same chair that had held Victoria's quivering body for most of the morning, and she began to read the day's news out loud.

Victoria, Elizabeth, Joseph and the old doctor stood assembled in the main kitchen of the mansion. It had been a hell of a night for all of them and it showed. Victoria had rested for most of the morning by her husband's bedside, and then finally retired to her rooms, leaving Elizabeth and Joseph to stand watch over Julian.

The doctor had arrived by early afternoon the following day to check on his patient. He had hoped to wake Julian in order to run some more tests but he hadn't had the heart to disturb Madison as she slept unknowingly by her dying father's side.

"I do think you should reconsider, Victoria," the old doctor persisted. "The end is approaching quickly now and it is no time for secrets. This is your family and friends we are talking about, your support system if you would just let them." He looked tired and had aged considerably since Julian's decline. He had grown to love the Carlton family as though it was his own and he loved Julian as the son he had never had. The old doctor would grieve long when Julian finally passed away.

"Please, I can't lie to him or your daughter any longer. This isn't the way to handle this, Victoria —"

"I understand your concern yet I must disagree. This secret has not spread beyond the persons in this room in over two years. That was my decision ever since the first day you came to me with my husband's diagnosis and will remain my course of action until I say otherwise. I will not have my household in mourning over a diagnosis and I will surely not have my friends pity me. Not to mention how the news will affect Madison and the wedding . . ." Exhaustion and sorrow were detectable in her voice yet her determination remained strong.

She would not inform her family or friends of her husband's unfortunate fate until after the merger of the Carlton and Leemon fortunes. She had to be the voice of reason in this madness, even as her heart broke. The pain in it felt like glass that had shattered into a million pieces and continued to stab and prick at her insides. And like glass, Victoria knew the sharpness of it would never dull.

She would lose her love and a great part of herself when Julian passed yet she would not forfeit her future, her life. She would not rest soundly until she watched her daughter wed the young Arthur Leemon in three weeks time. She depended on Madison and the merger now more than ever before. Only she could secure both their futures by making sure nothing got in the way of the wedding.

In the meantime, Victoria would continue to convince her dying husband that he was a healthy man, who had only recently suffered a slight setback which diet and exercise would surely remedy. Her guilt was easily overcome with determination and she drew her weary body up.

"Have I made myself clear?" She looked

over the small group until they all nodded in agreement. They were the only ones who knew the truth and would keep her secret a while longer.

"Good." She announced and exited the room with her head held high. She was doing the right thing and if she just kept focused on the prize, Victoria knew it would all pay off. She was powerless over Julian's disease and she would lose him. She had long accepted that. But she did have control over her future and she wasn't going to lose her dignity and the only lifestyle she had ever known.

Chapter Twenty

"Not much of a gymnast, are you, Blondie?"

Al carried a large sack over one muscular shoulder and held a rake in the other as she towered over Madison. Her head was covered with a blue bandana and her eyes hid behind mirrored sunglasses.

"I beg your pardon?" Madison asked. It was late summer and she was sitting by the pond typing away on her laptop computer when Al's cool voice interrupted her train of thought. She had a few more e-mails to write to some of her friends from college, with whom she would be traveling in September.

"By looking at you, I would have thought you'd be a little more limber. Scrawny arms explain why you can barely hold your own, ninety pounds is it?" Al smirked, removed her glasses and looked Madison dead in the eye. She was going to have a lot of fun with this one.

"I beg your pardon? Do you work here, Miss?"

"Nah, I just like carting around rakes and

work gloves for the hell of it. I know it must be shocking for a woman of your stature to regard another woman hard at work. God, you act like it's poison. It's just dirt."

The lean redhead looked amused as she picked at the dirt and grass stains on her shirt. Madison only stared back, open-mouthed and confused. She couldn't believe the utter rudeness of the young woman.

"Are you aware that I am a Carlton?"

"No shit? Jeez, and I thought you were the blonde here." Al acted surprised and as clueless as she could.

"I hope you know you are in violation of your contract because you are speaking to me. With that alone, you could lose your job and be expelled from these grounds for good."

"I thought you'd say that and it kind of reminds me of this guy I knew. Great crew worker, great arms — I'm sure you know the type. But it wasn't the talking that could have gotten him fired."

Understanding came over Madison's face and she diverted her eyes in shame.

"See you around, Blondie, and I suggest you get those arms in shape before your next urge strikes. Pulling a muscle over a one-story climb isn't doing much for my image around here."

Johnny came up the stone pathway that led to and surrounded the pond. It purposefully rounded itself entirely around the water and charmingly wove between the great willows that hung low and swayed lazily in the breeze.

He and Madison continued to meet only at night and as discreetly as possible, neither telling anyone about their meetings or growing love for each other.

Madison was already waiting for him when he arrived and the moon was high in the starlit sky. He came up to the iron bench that nestled quietly in the perfectly shadowed area of the pond. It was their favorite spot and had been as true to them all summer as they were to it. It cloaked them well and gave them the most wonderful view of the garden without the burden of the looming mansion in sight. They were entirely alone there and completely together.

He caught her sorrowful expression before she had seen him and brightened. He walked to her and, without a word, pulled her up on her feet and pressed soft, slow lips to hers. He wrapped his arms around her waist and whispered in her ear, "Hi beautiful, what were you thinking about?"

"Not much." She looked around, utterly

distracted. Her perfect face was now creased at the brow and frowned at the mouth with unhappiness. Her mind constantly wandered back to that afternoon and the unbelievably rude girl whom she hadn't even known worked for her father. And when she'd done some snooping, she'd been shocked to find out she was a veteran worker.

"Oh, come on. You look like you're trying to divide nine into one thousand and sixty-four. Now what's the real deal?" Johnny stepped back and held her at arm's length so he could get a look into her eyes.

She didn't know if she was ready to tell Johnny what had happened but he knew her so well and keeping secrets was starting to become impossible. She decided she didn't want more secrets between them and, unsure of how to tell him, she eased into it.

"I, uh . . . I met your friend. I think her name is Allison."

"Oh boy" was all he could manage. He rubbed his brow and took a seat, face in palms. He wondered what that girl was up to this time as his mind raced. She knew the rules as well as he did: no socializing with the employers. They all knew any communication went through Kay and even that was a very rare occasion. They did their work and stayed out of sight as much as possible. The more a Carlton got a look at you, the less likely you were coming back next season. And if crew weren't to be seen, well then they definitely weren't to be heard.

Johnny knew he was taking a huge risk with his career by being with Madison himself but he was willing to take that chance. He wondered what made it worth it for Al to break the house rules and take the same risk with her career.

"She's very beautiful. Did you guys have something? You know, were you ever involved?" Madison looked away, her voice was small but determined. She wanted him to answer her even though she wasn't sure she was prepared for the truth. His silence confirmed it.

"What did she have to say?" He turned the conversation and tried to sound light about it.

"Well, at first it wasn't what she said, but how she was saying it. She was rude and insulting. I don't like what she was implying about us, Johnny, and I think she's blackmailing me or something. What do you think she wants?" She tried to stay calm but she was already starting to understand what was really behind all of this — pure female jealousy; the worst kind.

"I don't know, princess. I really don't know." But he sure as hell was going to find out. He pulled her to him and his heart broke when she hung on like a scared puppy.

They were both taking a huge risk but somehow the burden of their love always fell more heavily on Madison.

"I don't know what's going on but I promise you it'll be okay," he said and she wanted more than anything to believe him.

"What's the deal, Allison, and do us both a favor and cut through the crap this time."

Johnny barged into Al's cabin early the next morning. He was furious and hated that he had to fight to keep his anger in check. He had had plenty of time to brood over the whole thing and the more he thought about it the more enraged he became. He could tell Al had really gotten to Madison and he hated that she was trying to come between them. Things were finally going alright for him and he wasn't going to let anyone screw it up.

Johnny knew Allison's mind and it was brilliant. What frightened him was that it was also calculating and devious. She was the most self-serving person he had ever known. And he knew she would do whatever it took to get what she wanted, even put her career and reputation on the line.

"What's with the formality, baby?" she asked innocently, though she had been expecting this exciting outburst from him. In fact, she'd been counting on it.

"I got a bone to pick with you."

"Oh yeah, well, I'm game for a little anything with you." She grinned and reached for the drawstring of his pants. He caught her at the wrist and added just enough pressure to have her eyes jump to his.

"Ahh, are you upset with me?" she whined and stared up at him through thick lashes. She leaned into him as he grasped her wrist.

So, he wants to play rough . . . she thought.

"You bet I am. What were you thinking talking to a Carlton? You know the rules, Al." He'd play her game and act like he was concerned for her job, not for her life.

"Oh, don't do that. It's insulting. I know you're getting your kicks off the old man's daughter. You don't have to dance around that with me. Now if Kay were here . . . then it would be another story."

"What is that, a threat?! What do you think you're doing, Allison? What game are you playing now?" His eyes filled with disgust and he hoped she didn't miss that either. She had to learn that manipulation wasn't going to get her anywhere with him. Maybe it had in the past but he was sorry for that now and knew he would never let her walk all over him again.

"Oh, cool it, will you? I was just having a little fun with the girl." She watched his eyes growing more and more impatient. "God, you act like you're in love with her," she spat and then pretended not to register his confirmation. "What's the matter? You don't want to share your new toy with your dear old friend?"

"You go too far, Allison. And anyway, three's a crowd. Sorry, but it looks like we still disagree on that one."

"I just hope you know what you're doing, slick. Girls like her are a little different from the girls you're used to. Just make sure you can handle the heat before you light the fire."

"I handled you just fine, though I wouldn't compare it to anything warm."

"Be careful, Johnny. That's all I'm preaching. You have no idea what you're getting yourself into. And you can trust me on that one."

Chapter Twenty-one

Madison took the day to pack for her trip. She no longer allowed Elizabeth to pack for her and hadn't since both women had gotten older. One old enough to select the perfect suit and shoe all on her own, the other old enough to fatigue at the mere thought of it.

Madison and five other friends from college were traveling to New York City to participate in the annual food drive that their school club sponsored for the homeless. Each year, the club raised money for the event and then hosted it in different cities throughout the country. A conference would follow the drive, where she and many other supporters from all over the nation would be joining the leaders of New York City for a discussion. She couldn't wait to get her say in. When it came to saving the world, Madison never held anything back. She gained a confidence when she fought for what she believed in, and felt she resembled her father when she got down to business. She was proud of that and fed off the high she got from all of it. She was hardly a ball of nerves when it came to standing up for those who couldn't defend themselves.

When she was done packing, she took a few minutes to review her notes and felt the excitement rise in her stomach. The summer had raced by and it was time to get back into her routine. She just loved seeing the faces of those who had nothing when she handed them a bagful of groceries and clothing.

She'd be gone a week but Madison knew that her fight wouldn't be over once she left New York City. Once she returned home, the real battle would begin. She planned to tell her father she was calling off the wedding to Arthur Leemon. She would use the courage she would gain at the conference and stand up to her father upon her return. She hadn't wanted to upset him since his illness in August but since then, he had recovered fully. He was back to his old self and business as usual and she couldn't hold off the merger any longer. She would tell him everything. She would tell him that she was in love.

"Come on, princess, just a hint. Where are you taking me?"

"I want to show you something," Madison answered him slyly and kissed his cheek. The look in her eyes had her promising another and all he had to do to get it was follow her.

She led him from the pond's end where they had met that night and headed west into the thick of strong-smelling trees that surrounded the orchards. They were designed to act as a beautiful lush fence, keeping hungry animals out and protecting the glorious fruit trees of their world-famous orchards.

After snagging a midnight snack off a low branch, Johnny continued to follow close behind her along the shadowed shrubs. When he had lost her in the darkness, he only had to close his eyes and follow the sweet scent of lilacs and baby powder.

Madison finally stopped at the northwest corner then slipped through the hedge and out from behind the orchard's shield.

"Here," she whispered and gestured to the thick door of yet another of the mansion's side entrances.

"Are you crazy?"

"It's the library and an extension off the main house. They'll never hear us. Please, I want to show you something." He still looked weary so she took the lead and pushed hard against the massive door. It wasn't used much and she had often forgotten it was even there.

When it finally gave, they entered the dark room hand-in-hand. And when she broke away, leaving him standing in the enormous blackness, only the smell of old books to guide him, he tensed.

"You better not be looking for the light switch."

"Way ahead of you," she answered and sparked a match to ignite the chorus of candles that lined the stone fireplace.

"Wow," was all he could say and think of. "This is really something." Johnny spun in slow circles, trying to take it all in.

The ceilings soared and the wall-shelves seemed to go on forever. Cozy armchairs and couches invited anyone to pick up a book and snuggle up by the huge hearth.

He watched her scan the endless bookcases and her eyes finally fall on an old, tattered leather-bound novel. She passed it to him without a word and waited.

"What's this?" The gold writing of the title had been worn away and Johnny had to gently open it, careful not to let any of the loose pages spill to the floor, so he could read the first line.

"Twain's *The Adventures of Tom Sawyer and Huckleberry Finn*? I don't understand."

"It's my favorite book. Always has been, as you can tell. My father used to read it to me, a little every night, and Elizabeth would continue on the nights when father was too busy. But somehow, we always got through it and when we did, I would make them start all over again from the beginning. I wanted to memorize it so I could replay the story in my head. Then when I learned to read, there were so many other books to enjoy, I guess I just forgot all about Huck and his adventures.

"He reminds me of you, the courageous and free-spirited boy who has seen and done so much and will forever more because it's who he is. We do have something in common, only I just read and dream about it; you live it."

"Funny, I never read much. They never cared to force us in public school, but I did read this one. And of my own free will, that's the best time to do something, when you want to. Freedom, even if it's just as simple as the books you choose to read." He reached for her hand and kissed it, turning it over, making sure he didn't miss one inch of her.

"I used to lay out flat on my belly on that rug right over there and watch the flames dance over the pages. Still do when I get a chance. Want to join me?"

Her eyes sparkled in the soft candlelight and he thought he saw the adventurous child in her from so many years ago shining through.

"Yeah, I'd join you anywhere."

She smiled to herself as she remembered the reluctance on his face, only minutes ago, when she had invited him into the library.

They snuggled close together on the large rug and Johnny draped an old afghan around their shoulders.

"It's chilly in here without the fire . . ." she observed.

"Don't even think about it. I'll keep you warm," he said, worried that someone might find them there. He lowered his mouth to hers and waited for her to close the gap. Her lips were so soft he could hardly believe he had gone so long without knowing them.

"I'm going to miss you when you're gone," he admitted.

"It'll only be a week."

"If it were only a day it would be too long."

"God, where do you get this stuff from?"

"Charm school, now kiss me again."

And she did, but with more energy than he had ever felt from her before. She seemed to search deeper and deeper until she had him on his knees, feeling for something to brace himself against. But Madison had other plans. With effortless strength, she had him flat on his back and hardly noticing the coldness of the rug. She was reaching for the buttons on her sweater and cursing the lot of them when Johnny's surprise turned to laughter.

"Now why would I ever buy a sweater with this many buttons?" she cursed herself under her breath.

"I thought you were cold?"

"Yes, I was, very. But you are doing such a fine job of warming me up. Now shut up and help me! When I get this thing off, it'll be the last time."

"Well, in that case, let me show you how it's done."

With one strong index finger, Johnny had the rest of the stubborn sweater buttons hitting the library's floor.

"My hero," she teased but the gleam in her eye had Johnny sure that she wasn't joking anymore.

Madison's face had turned serious and her actions slowed from her initial frenzy to sensual, ritualistic movements.

She slowly reached for the collar of his shirt and stared straight into his eyes.

"I want to see you now."

Barely able to control himself, Johnny had

to force himself not to rip his own shirt in two. As the candlelight flickered over them, Johnny brought his arms over his head to remove his shirt and expose the soft skin and hard muscle of his bare chest.

"You're so beautiful," she gasped.

"That's supposed to be my line," he joked nervously. He had never seen her this serious before or her eyes so heavy.

Soon, she was caressing his shoulders and chest and her soft lips fluttered over every inch of his body. The pads of her fingers glided over the long mounds of his tense muscle.

"Relax, lay back and close your eyes," she told him and waited for him to do so.

He felt her mouth kiss his forehead and then his nose and mouth. She stayed there a while, sucking his top lip and then bottom, and then moved to his chin and neck, where she took her time to feel and lick and tickle. His fists bunched in her hair in response. He was so aroused now he had to fight to control himself and she knew she was driving him mad.

"Relax, enjoy, we have all night," she reminded him and continued down his chest, kissing and kneading and licking and sucking at the tough muscle and delicate skin. She slid her body over his as she moved farther down and could feel his growing desire for her press into her belly.

She had never been this sensual or domineering before but the role seemed to fit perfectly. She normally played the passive type who never let the kiss go too long or get too hot, but tonight was different. Tonight she was ready and was slowly losing all control of her inhibitions. Tonight she was a woman in love and in desire with Johnny Sparks and she wanted to spend the next hours showing him how much she truly wanted him.

"You don't have to do this, Madison —"

"Shh, I want to. I want you . . ." she answered and began tugging on the waist of his jeans. "Don't you want me?"

"Yeah —"

"Good, now shut up and lay back."

The candles flickered around them and the endless rows of books enclosed them. They were all alone, free to do what they pleased, and both of them wanted this night to go on forever. In the morning, everything would be back to normal, back to the secrets and lies and stolen nights and embraces, but tonight their love was celebrated. Tonight their love was real, tangibly undeniable, and both of them were finding it hard to contain themselves.

"I love you, Madison."

"I know."

And when they were finally freed of all their clothing, Johnny wrapped his arms around her bare back and turned gently to lay her on the rug. She looked like an angel and for a second Johnny didn't want to continue.

"What's wrong?" she asked after a moment.

"You're perfect," he said and waited for her to let him know what to do next. With wide eyes, she slowly nodded and pulled him down to her. He slipped inside her and a slight gasp escaped her lips.

"Are you okay?"

She nodded yes and moved her hips slowly, discovering this new sensation that was instantly warming her insides. She could feel everything, his breath on her neck, his beating heart, and she could feel him throbbing inside her. Tears sprang to her eyes as a new revelation came over her.

"Are you okay? Why are you crying? Does it hurt?" he asked and kissed her tears.

"We fit." She wanted to scream it but could only get her voice to hum it and Johnny was relieved and thrilled for their new discovery.

"I know we do. We will always fit."

"I love you so much."

He nodded seriously, understanding the magnitude of her confession. He had thought she might but had never heard it from her lips until now. And surprisingly, he wasn't even a little scared, only honored and a little more hopeful for their future.

"Now it's your turn to relax." He gestured for her to lay her head back and close her eyes. Once she did, he began the slow, fluid movements that made them both soar to new heights. When he gently brought her to the edge, pleasure ripped through her and she shed tears of joy once again.

When they were finally exhausted and wrapped in each other's arms, Johnny made his last plea: "Don't go."

"Stop that; I have to. They need me."

"But you said you went last year. I bet they'd understand."

"They probably would, as a matter of fact. I am the only one who goes every year, but that's not the point. My parents wouldn't. They'd think something was wrong. They'd be suspicious."

"So what's wrong with that? They must be suspicious already. You are positively glowing, princess. Tell me they haven't noticed you floating on air all month long?"

The truth was they had yet, conveniently,

everyone just assumed she was excited about her marriage to Arthur.

"It's just not a good time, okay?"

"So when is? Are you ever going to tell them about us?"

"Just let me handle this, please?"

"Fine, okay, I give up. You know them better than I do. I just don't know how long I can go on being your mistress."

"Oh, come on, you like being my secret love affair in the woods. Admit it."

"You're wrong, I love it. I'm still not convinced you have to go the city though," he began pouting again and she kissed him hard to shut him up.

Chapter Twenty-two

Al completed her workout that night with a light jog through the forest. She had discovered a beaten dirt path that led through the woods during her first year on hire at the mansion but she had never felt inclined to use it until now. She had had a couple of restless nights lately and she suspected she knew the cause. Johnny Sparks had been on her mind more than usual and with the merciless humidity hanging all around, she found herself clouded with desire for him. And she just hated having an itch she couldn't scratch.

She finished up her jog and headed to her cabin to towel down. The night was growing hotter as an Indian summer seemed to weigh heavily over them. She stopped to look out over the illuminated gardens that spread endlessly before her.

Al sucked in the thick air, feeling unusually full and warm inside. It seemed to fill her lungs, her head and her heart began to pound all over again. She closed her eyes at the utter pleasure of it and the rush of blood booming throughout her swelling body had her remembering Johnny and what she wanted — no, needed — from him.

She quickly forgot about heading to her own cabin for a shower and turned towards the softly lit window of Johnny's instead. She came up to his cabin and became instantly dizzy from its sharp aroma. Heat swelled on the back of her neck, creeping down over her shoulders and breasts as her chest heaved and sucked the air. Her entire body was damp and when she kicked off her runners, she felt the soft grass sweating between her toes. The sharp green of her piercing stare had clouded over and her lids were heavy.

Al nudged the heavy door open and was delighted to hear the shower running in the next room. She was ravaged with want for him and had to keep herself from tearing at her wet clothes.

The small bath was devoured in steam and she could hardly make him out through it all. Hot and steamy, just the way she liked it.

Her drenched tank and shorts slid off her glistening body in the soft glow of the room and she stepped soundlessly into the hard spray of the shower.

"Just what I needed after a hard workout,"

she purred dreamily and, after a long look over Johnny's rock hard body, she tilted her head back into the scalding water, exposing an arching throat and heaving chest.

Johnny was far from surprised at his new guest. It wasn't the first time Al had made a play for him since she'd found out he was seeing Madison.

He watched her body moved rhythmically closer and closer to his and then felt the drag of her impatient claws across his swollen muscles. He dipped his head forward, letting the water drown him. He knew what she wanted from him, the one thing she had always and only wanted.

He thought about the irony of it all as she pressed her aching body against his. He had loved her years ago, a young and innocent love that only a first can be. And she had used him, all the while guarding her heart against love and waiting for a change in the breeze to take her off to somewhere new, into someone else's arms. Now, it seemed, the breeze only brought her back to him. But this time he was stronger, he was in love, with life and with Madison Carlton. It was exhilarating and wonderful and Al didn't stand a chance against any of it.

He clasped a hand around her inviting throat and pinned her back up against the cool tiled wall. Her eyes fluttered opened in shock and he took one last look into them.

He grinned slowly and closed his mouth over hers. She began to melt under the pressure of him but he broke away just as quickly as he had pinned her. And just as he had expected, he felt nothing.

Smiling like a fool, he shoved the soap in her groping hands and left her to enjoy the only person she truly ever could — herself.

"He's taken a turn, Victoria. There's not much I can do at this point besides ease the pain." The doctor's voice was grave and the news tore at his heart even as he reported it.

The last couple of years had been torture as he witnessed the descent of his good friend's health. The last couple of months had been worse as the disease struck down mercilessly. He couldn't stand it anymore. He would no longer lie to his dying friend. He would give him answers and support and reassurance. And if Julian so desired, he would promise to watch over his precious daughter, Madison.

"But there must be, Doctor. I . . . we can't lose him now; it's too soon. You have to give me more time!" Victoria pleaded with the old man.

"There is no more time. And no more lies.

Do you understand me, woman?" He feared she had gone hysterical and he had to be firm with her.

The glare she shot him had him signing a sedative prescription for her and leaving Elizabeth with the unenviable job of calming her down.

When the doctor left, Victoria paced like a caged tiger in the darkened study. Her black curls were wild and her hands wrung at each other until they were red and raw. She had to re-evaluate her situation now that Julian's condition had worsened drastically. Madison was away, thank God, and the merger wasn't for another week. She was trapped and she felt it now, looking into Elizabeth's eyes. Time was her enemy and she had to devise a plan that would defeat even that. If she could not secure her name to the Leemon fortune before her husband died, she would have nothing.

Madison, being the only heir of the Carlton fortune, would inherit it all and, even then, only upon marriage. Knowing her daughter, the fortune would quickly be turned into a charity fund for starving children in faraway places. She had to get her hands into the Leemon fortune to protect her own future. She had no choice. And she wouldn't rest until her daughter was married.

"Madison, darling, you must return home at once. I have the most wonderful news. The wedding has been pushed up and you are getting married the day after tomorrow. Isn't that wonderful?"

Victoria's sweetest voice waited for her daughter to respond on the other end of the telephone. They were running out of time and every moment that insisted to pass made her more and more nervous. Julian was now bedridden and she had to act fast. This long-distance phone call was step one in her new plan.

"Mother, is everything all right?" Madison asked after a few recovery seconds. She had been preparing for dinner in New York City when the unexpected call came through from the hotel's operator.

"Nothing could be more right," Victoria lied. "You'll come home immediately and we'll have a celebration unlike all the rest." Her voice was cheery and fake and Madison saw right through it. Something was up but she knew she'd never get the truth from her mother. Madison had noticed how her mother had slowly become as hard as a rock over the past few years and that was part of the reason why they had had such a detached relationship lately, even though they were mother and daughter.

"Could you put Elizabeth on the phone, Mother? I'd like to hear how she's doing," Madison asked suspiciously. It saddened her that she felt this way about her own mother but the whole situation was sounding very odd.

"No, no, darling. You can speak to her when you arrive home. Now have a safe trip and we'll see you soon." The line disconnected then, leaving Madison confused and deeply disturbed.

Something was very wrong; she knew it, and she was going to get herself home as quickly as possible so she could get the real story. She would have plenty of time to battle with government wars once she called off the wedding and proposed to the man she truly loved. Life would be so different with Johnny. It would finally be hers. Madison couldn't wait for her new life and, for the first time in a long time, she was excited about her future.

Chapter Twenty-three

Elizabeth was waiting by the mansion's main entrance when Madison's car pulled up. She had overheard Victoria's phone conversation and wondered what she was up to. She would have liked a warning that the child was arriving home early, since she was the one who was going to be doing the explaining and then the comforting, but that wasn't Victoria's style. Cool and calm was her style, intriguing some might have called it, but Elizabeth preferred to refer to it as insensitive.

At least she had finally agreed to inform Julian about the truth of his condition, she thought. What made Elizabeth suspicious was the sudden rush on the wedding. She was going to find out why Victoria had gone to all the trouble to reschedule, especially when Julian had fallen ill again. But first she had to think of Madison. She'd be telling her the truth about her father's condition and she wasn't going to hold anything back. If they were going to marry the girl off like she was a grown woman then she was going to start treating her like one too. And this young woman deserved to know the truth, as awful as it was, and Elizabeth knew Madison was grown up enough to understand and handle herself. All the same, she certainly didn't want the cool storytelling of her mother or the shock of hearing it from her father. Elizabeth volunteered herself for the monumental task, just as she had done on so many other occasions in Madison's life. She would tell Madison that her father was dying.

The driver parked and came around to open the door. Madison stepped out with the grace of a queen and let herself be escorted up and into the mansion's entrance.

She was put together impeccably and her face was as hard and serious as stone. Elizabeth startled at what she saw. Her little Madison looked all grown up and all of a sudden it was hard to remember the pigtails and pink flannel jumpsuits.

Madison wore a black designer suit that morning and her blonde hair was pulled tightly back and knotted into a simple bun at the nape of her long neck. Her face was lightly dusted with blush and eye shadow but it was obvious that Madison had had little time to bother with anything fancy. Her eyes looked more focused on other things and her mouth was pressed into a determined line. She wanted answers to her suspicions and had a few answers of her own to give her parents about what she had been up to all summer. Determination turned her eyes to ice; she was ready to pick up the phone and tell Arthur and the Leemons that she wouldn't marry him herself if she had to.

Elizabeth thought Madison looked drained and defeated for a moment as she watched her climb the marble staircase. Yet once she reached her old friend, Madison stood tall, confident and strong, despite the fact that her eyes threatened to water at the sight of Elizabeth's concerned expression.

The worry and wonder of a thousand questions lay on Madison's pale cheeks and her imploring stare made it obvious she wasn't going to put up with being lied to any longer. They were going to listen to her now because she had the most powerful weapon on her side: she was a woman in love and she knew exactly what she wanted. That alone made her invincible.

Madison embraced Elizabeth quickly, lingering a moment in the softness of her sturdy arms and then straightened.

"We have much to discuss. Meet me in the library in half an hour," she informed Elizabeth with a serious air and then headed up the main stairs to her suite.

"Yes. Yes, we do, my child."

Madison reached the end of the hallway and could smell her quarters before she even reached their doors. She breathed in heavily and recognized the scent immediately. Closing her eyes, she was instantly standing by the pond's end, dancing slowly to that wonderful waltz under the wide open sky. She hummed and smiled, forgetting all about her troubles as her tense shoulders relaxed.

Parting the heavy doors, she stepped inside and nearly lost her room in the colors and scents of hundreds of blooming flowers. A shaky hand covered her gaping mouth as she laughed out loud and quite uncontrollably.

Giddy with surprise and dazed from the wonderful smell, Madison maneuvered herself past the front hall and into her bedroom. Her eyes shone wide with amazement when she found more glorious colors and scents and, finally, the simple note pinned to the balcony's rail.

Awaiting your return with the patience of a gardener.
Oh yeah, and I love you.

Tears spilled over her smiling cheeks as Elizabeth entered.

"How could he have? How did he know that I was coming home early?"

"It was I. I told him. He was hanging around your balcony like a lovesick puppy dog. I had to have a talk with the poor lad."

"So you know." She didn't ask but simply stated the words after a minute's time.

"Yes, my dear, that I do. But I will tell you, it wasn't news to me. You are more to me than any daughter could be. You are part of me, just as your papa is. Where did you suppose you got such a heart from? A romantic heart may be a curse but it's gotten me along just fine, and you too I can see." She gestured to the room and smiled. "He loves you so much and seeing your face just now, I know you love him too."

Madison flew into Elizabeth's arms and held on tight. They were both sobbing now and Madison realized that the warm feeling spreading though her body was the assurance and the support she so desperately needed. She hated all the sneaking around, the constant deceiving of her parents. It had all felt so deviant for so long but denying her feelings for Johnny had been a torture she couldn't bear.

"I know what I have to do." Madison

broke away and wiped at her face. She had gathered her strength and it was time to make everything right.

"Yes, and you will. But right now I have something to tell you before you see your parents." Elizabeth braced herself for what was to come. She wished things were different, that she could make all the hurt go away like she had the nightmares and skinned knees.

"Your papa is —"

"Good morning, Madison! Well, well, what is all this?" Victoria breezed into the foyer and then into the bedroom. She gasped and looked around in awe.

"That Arthur is quite the romantic. I just spoke with him yesterday. Oh, the lengths he must have gone to having had all of these beautiful flowers delivered in such little time." She blushed as she remembered all the glorious things power and money could do.

"I'll call him right away and thank him for his efforts. Spoiling our bride-to-be may become a wonderful new pastime for him, with enough positive reinforcement of course."

Madison's eyes narrowed on her mother. Victoria never burst into a room unannounced and her voice now uncharacteristically boomed. Blood-red lipstick painted an exaggerated smile on her lips and her dark curls were drawn back into a tight twist, revealing dangerously high cheekbones and darting black eyes. Madison watched her mother closely, both surprised and suspicious at the unusual display before her.

Victoria brought her face to a magnificent lily in full bloom and caught a glimpse of what she supposed was the greeting card from the splendid person who had arranged all of this. The simple slip was dull compared to the scene surrounding them and only Madison recognized that it was the same paper Johnny used for his sketches. Slipping it out from under her mother's prying eyes, she felt the thickness of it between her fingers and remembered how much she loved and missed him. The flowers had made her smile but this little scrap of paper was part of him and rubbing it felt like running her fingers over his supple skin.

Victoria watched her daughter's eyes grow misty as she clung to the small note. Madison was never misty-eyed over anything to do with Arthur Leemon. Warning bells went off inside Victoria's aching head and in an instant she was lunging forward and snatching at the little note. Madison was too slow.

And at that moment, Madison knew it was all over. She turned and closed the balcony doors and then headed towards the hall to seek out her father as her mother pored over the precious note. It was now or never.

". . . of a gardener? And I love you!" Victoria's voice rose to a high-pitched shrill as she read what Johnny had scribbled for Madison. Understanding had come quick to Victoria's mind and she turned to her daughter's departing back. "You little tramp, how could you?" she growled harshly and then quickly recovered her poise.

"Madison." Her mother's voice was instantly firm and unusually calm.

Madison stopped at the threshold of her quarters, a steady hand on the door's frame.

"He's dying, Madison. He'll be gone in a couple days' time." Victoria let herself flop into the chair she had been standing beside. She grinned as she spoke and by the time she was done, she was snorting with laughter at herself as though fate had played a cruel joke that only the defeated could find humor in.

Madison turned to face the chilling laughter and found her mother's expression haunting. Her chillingly dark eyes gazed off into nothing in particular, as though she

161

were talking to herself or someone no one else could see. When she finally composed herself, Victoria looked up into her daughter's stunned face and smiled again with complete satisfaction.

"You will do as your father wanted and you will marry whom he has chosen for you. You will do him that much honor. You always were a good girl, Daddy's little girl," she mocked her daughter, looking pleased at her prediction of the impending future.

She knew Madison well; they all did. The obedient girl would do exactly as her father wished, especially now. Madison would marry Arthur Leemon no matter how much her heart detested it and Victoria was finally home-free. Her exhausted body relaxed at the mere thought of it. After losing so much, victory was finally hers.

"I don't believe you" was all Madison said as she turned and stepped into the long hall. She tried to stay calm as she hurried down the stairs but her fears caught in her throat as she remembered her father, still and gray, after he had suffered a stroke.

More lies, she thought as she ran down the hallway to the sick room. She prayed she would find the small room empty but she called out and threw open the heavy door all the same.

"Daddy? . . . Daddy?" She searched for signs of her mother's lie and found only the horrible truth.

Chapter Twenty-four

Julian lay unconscious in the narrow bed. Machinery was set up now all around him, monitoring his existence. Dutifully, they beeped and hummed, recording every breath and heartbeat, and waiting patiently for the last.

He was heavily sedated with strong pain-killers and, as a result, slipped in and out of consciousness without realizing it. He was calm and comfortable and ready.

"Daddy?" Madison stood in the dark doorway, unable to enter the stuffy room. It was all too much to take in. Her grief-stricken soul struggled to believe what her eyes and ears beheld. It still felt as though she were fighting her way out of a horrible nightmare. She hadn't even recognized her own voice. Her head swam and the air suffocated her, like two strong hands squeezing her throat, until she had to gulp at the air between sobs to breathe. The oak doorframe was all that kept her standing upright.

When Julian soundlessly stirred after

some time, Madison finally released the doorframe and crossed the room to him. She had lost; this was real. Her mother had finally told the truth, though she had obviously kept this truth a lie for some time.

It was shocking to see how pale and thin he had grown since she last saw him earlier in the week. If his physical depletion had been a gradual descent over the months, she had hardly noticed the effects until now.

"Oh, Daddy. Why?" She watched him closely at first and then reached out and placed a shaky hand on his. It was so hot she had to pull hers away and new panic rose in her belly. She dashed to the small closet and pulled out as many face towels as she could find. One by one, she dunked them into the pitcher of ice water that stood untouched by his bedside. Her hands were soon blue and painful from the cold as she draped the frigid cloths over her father's forehead, neck, chest and arms. He hadn't moved or responded to the cold on his body and within seconds the towels were warm again.

Tears burned in Madison's eyes as she frantically re-submerged the towels and prayed for someone to help her. She was fighting a losing battle and couldn't stop herself when she finally realized she was powerless against his raging fever and impending death.

The old doctor arrived then and found a hysterical Madison bent over her father's unresponsive body. He knew the time would come when she would find out the truth. In fact, he had insisted upon it, hadn't he? But his heart ached over the sight of her pain. She was so young and so innocent and she hadn't suspected a thing for two long years. In that time, he had longed to tell her before it came to this, but time had run out for both of them. Victoria had been adamant and frightfully determined to do it her way. The old doctor scolded himself now for being such a fool, such a coward.

Madison caught movement in the corner of her eye and turned her head to find the old doctor staring at her from the doorway.

"He's too hot; you have to help me." Her plea came in heaving sobs and she looked at him with desperation as she continued to replace the warming towels with icy ones.

"Please, he's burning up! You have to stop this, please. You're killing him!"

"No, there is nothing we can do for him now. His body is having a natural reaction. He's still fighting this. This wasn't a surprise to us; we've known for some time, Madison.

I'm so sorry to admit that to you now . . . I am so sorry. I was a coward. Please forgive me."

"No, you bastard! You're lying; you're all lying!" she screamed harder and louder as the doctor struggled to take the ice water away from her. As she continued her screeching, her throat began to sound as raw as her hands looked.

"Leave me alone and help him! You don't know what you're talking about. No, please don't . . . I have to cool him down . . . He's too hot. Can't you see that?"

"Madison, darling, we've done all we can for him; now we wait. Leave that to his body, Madison."

He finally managed to pry the dripping cloths from her shaking hands. "And just talk to him. This is beyond the body, Madison. You must tend to his soul now."

He sat her down slowly into the chair beside Julian's bed and left her to weep into her raw hands. She collapsed and the overstuffed cushions engulfed her. He checked the monitors for Julian's vital signs and took his temperature one last time and then left Madison alone to say good-bye to her father. He would advise Elizabeth to summon the priest within the hour. Julian was ready for his last rites.

* * *

So her mother hadn't been lying — not about this. Damn it! Deep within her, Madison needed this to be fake, just a horrible nightmare conjured up by Victoria. She sat back in the oversized armchair and stared out the tiny window of the sick room. The machines beeped and hummed all around her until the sounds matched the rhythm of her pounding head. She was alone with her thoughts and her dying father.

In her contemplation, she wondered where everyone else was and then realized she didn't really care. Her father was dying and they — all of them — had kept it from her. They'd even allowed her to leave home when he had been so dangerously ill, all the while covering up their mourning and the truth with silly plans for a wedding. Ridiculous, she thought, and shameful.

She tried to remember back to the last time she had shared a lunch or more than a couple of words with him. She had been so caught up in Johnny and her trip that the entire summer hardly held a memory of her precious father. At the thought, she instantly hated herself as panic rose again in her throat. What if she couldn't remember him when he was gone? His voice, his laughter, his words that were always so honest and full of wisdom and love?

Tears began to fall again without her consent, without her knowledge. She felt so far away from the two men she adored and incapable of reaching either one of them. The sadness was too much as she realized she was losing one forever. The only consolation was the silent vow she made to herself, promising that she would not lose the other, no matter what.

Madison wished she could tell her father all about her new life, the one she had cowardly hidden from him, and everyone else, for months. All she wanted now was to make her father understand what she was feeling and so she did as the old doctor suggested: she spoke to him.

Her quivering voice was no more than a whisper when the words finally left her lips. And with those words, all the fear and shame left as well, lifting a heavy weight from Madison's shoulders.

"Daddy, I met a wonderful man this spring. You don't know him or his family but his name is Johnny Sparks and he is one of our ground workers. You've already signed him on for another season. Isn't that impressive? He's done wonders for the garden and in such a short time. And I can hardly tell you the wonders he has shown me this summer. But I'm going to try. No more lies." She took a deep breath and scolded herself when she realized she was still speaking from her head.

"No more lies," she repeated and this time spoke from her heart. "Daddy, I've fallen in love with a wonderful man this summer. He fills every emptiness my heart has ever felt until it's bursting with joy and acceptance and love. He calms my fears and celebrates my hopes and dreams, without even knowing what a precious gift it is to me. He has taught me to live each day on the breath of its immense glory and the promise of tomorrow's.

"I know he loves me. I've never been more sure of anything in my entire life. And the thought of facing another day without his contagious laugh or encouragement or spontaneous embraces sends horrible aches through my heart. I never thought it would be, but love is scary and wonderful and enlightening all at once. It has allowed me to discover things about myself and my capacity to love. And just when I think I love him enough to burst the very seams of my heart, I wake up to a new morning and find I've found one more glorious inch, and another reason to hang on and never let go."

She was smiling through her tears as memories of Johnny's wide smile and laughing eyes danced through her head and then an enormous wave of guilt managed to drown the happiness in her heart with one quick downpour.

"I truly wish I could have loved who you've chosen for me. I feel ungrateful and a liar and a cheat when I think about all the time and faith you put into this arrangement. I tried, Daddy, I really did. But I'm not sorry for my actions. This summer has been the best time of my life because of one awesome person. You created my life, a very wonderful one, and now Johnny has changed it. He's the one for me; my heart knows it. And I want you to be as happy for me as I am.

"I've upset mother already with the truth and many more people will be hurt shortly. I am sorry for that. All I really care about now are your feelings. Don't hate me, God. Please don't hate me. I couldn't bear it; I couldn't live with myself . . . If you wish me to marry Arthur, I will. If you want our fortune to continue to serve the family then that is what I will do with it. I love you so much. Elizabeth told me that we share the same heart — a romantic one —"

Madison had to stop now. Her heart had

begun a horrible ache at the thought of giving up Johnny and losing her father and every one of her hopes and dreams all at once. Her trembling hands held her tear-streaked face, covering the pain in her eyes, shielding the dark reality that lay before her. She bowed her head and sobbed quietly.

"I think . . . she's right . . . about that . . . my darling." Julian's eyes remained closed and his body so still that Madison was sure she had only imagined the sweet huff of her father's voice.

"All . . . I've . . . ever wanted . . . was for you . . . to be happy," he began again with unbelievable strain.

Madison was on her feet now and her blue eyes sparkled like diamonds through her tears.

"Daddy? Oh God, all I've ever wanted was for you to be proud of me. I didn't know you were sick, Daddy, really I didn't."

"Neither . . . did I," he huffed. "Your mother . . . was trying . . . to protect us."

"But they lied to us and robbed us of so much time," Madison replied defiantly.

Julian opened his eyes then and saw his little girl then for the first time in a long time. She looked wronged and angry and he realized that she was still so young. He saw now what he himself had robbed his little girl of and it was much. He wanted to make it up to her and he would.

"You'll have . . . to take care . . . of her now. Your . . . mother needs you . . . even if she can't tell you."

"I will, of course. And Elizabeth and Joseph and . . ."

"And Johnny and Madison," his voice grew stronger now.

"What? Oh, yes, of course." Madison's body was overcome with sobs as she gathered her father's withering body in her arms. She could hardly believe her ears. He had heard every word. "Yes, I will."

"You must fight, Madison. For what you want . . . for what you believe in. You're a fighter . . . just like me. If you had told me sooner . . . I don't know what I would have done . . . But that's all over now," he whispered through a struggling smile.

The old doctor, Victoria, Elizabeth, Joseph and the community priest stood in the dark doorway, silently staring. None of them had the heart to interrupt Julian's dying words.

"Madison will marry . . . whom she chooses or none at all, if the case may be. The fortune will be left in her capable hands . . . to do with as she pleases," Julian announced.

Everyone nodded in understanding and Madison flew into Elizabeth's arms as Julian slipped back into unconsciousness. The priest prepared for the last rites ceremony.

Chapter Twenty-five

Al grinned widely to herself as she removed buckets of built-up algae from the pond's oxygen pump earlier that day. She had actually lost the draw and was now knee-deep in the annual battle of man versus the disgusting, multiplying micro-organisms of the Carlton pond.

Rubber overalls and green goo couldn't touch her good mood with a ten-foot pole. She simply radiated with self-satisfaction. By the way Johnny had fallen headfirst into oblivion earlier in the week, she was sure little-miss-perfect had finally left for her important meeting. And, by the way he was suddenly resurfacing like a shiny new penny, Al suspected they were all to anticipate her return very shortly.

But whatever her majesty had to do over in New York City couldn't have been so important if the entire trip had only taken three days. Al wasn't complaining though. She had a plan, a delicious plan, and Madison's early return only kick-started it into action. It was time to tell Romeo that his precious Juliet was a lying, spoiled brat. If Kay couldn't break it to him, she would. Either way, she could hardly wait for Johnny to hear the exciting news. They were all in for a day off, direct orders from the missus herself, as the garden was to play host to a wedding the following day.

Al licked the curve of her chapped lips. Johnny was really going to trip when he heard the truth about Madison. Her tanned arms flexed in the rising sunlight, proving that she was ready to catch him when he did. Johnny would be hers again and knowing it caused a sinfully hot pleasure to run through her veins.

"Hey, Al. You gonna have that wrapped up by noon?" Kay asked. He was doing the rounds, checking up on all the sections into which he had divided the massive grounds. He needed everything done and all signs of the doers gone within the hour. Mrs. Carlton might be a piece to look at but his brief meeting with her earlier in the day had proved that if you looked too long you were likely to get burned by her temper. She was in some mood and Kay quickened his step at the thought of it. He was going to do his job and then get himself and his crew the hell out of her way.

"Yah, yah. I'll be done in ten," Al answered flatly, annoyed that Kay had interrupted her wild and wonderful fantasies.

"Okay, good. It all looks good. No, it looks great Al and the orchards are trimmed and the morning's leaves have been cleared and . . ."

"Hey, one too many cups this morning, boss?" He was pacing and sweating and really getting in the way of her cleanup.

"Nah, I'm just nervous over this whole business. Mrs. Carlton sure put a flame under my ass this morning." He lifted his old baseball cap and dragged a tense hand through his wet hair.

"Yeah, those Carlton women can have that effect on a guy," she said blandly and sent a knowing looking over her shoulder.

"About the grounds, Red. And it's not just that. Johnny's gonna freak when I tell him to pack it up early today as none of us were invited to his girlfriend's wedding tomorrow.

"Look," he continued when Al simply shrugged, obviously a little less than interested in his dilemma, "I just don't want to lose him. The kid's got talent. He's the best I've had around here in years." Kay's brown eyes were so honest Al had to look away.

"Hey, what's that supposed to mean?"

She recovered smoothly with a teasing look of hurt.

"You know what I mean. You know him good, right?"

Allison nodded noncommittally and had to suppress a whistle. If he only knew how well . . .

"How about you help him out when the news hits, okay? And no funny business, Ace; he's gonna need a friend. Nothing more. He's a good kid; let's try to help him out. Things will probably get hairy around here once he finds out about —"

"Okay, okay. He'll be fine, Kay. I'll make sure of it. Now scram before I get your hot ass in here with me to cool off."

Every member of the Carlton household and a few close friends stood assembled to say their good-byes to Julian. He had passed away peacefully and though it had come as a surprise to most of the mourners, they understood that he had suffered a terrible disease for years and that his final sleep was a blessing.

The minutes that passed were bittersweet for Madison. She had lost so much in the past day yet she had received the power to control the rest of her life in return. She remembered the precious few words her father spoke to her just moments before he died. As long as she fought, she would never really lose him. Her confidence and strength was in him and his memory, and she need only stand up for herself and what she wanted and believed in to feel him close to her. That was a gift she would cherish forever.

Her tears had stopped as she had ceased mourning her loss. She now praised her father's memory and all that he had left them with. And when the sad guests began to leave, Madison called a much needed family meeting.

She had a lot to tell them all and it was time she assumed the responsibility that was now hers. She was head of the household now and though Julian had left enormous shoes to fill, Madison only needed to look to her strength within to fill them.

"I stand here now, before all of you, as the new head of the Carlton household," she began when everyone was assembled. She hadn't prepared a speech and decided she'd simply speak from her heart. "I knew this day would come yet I never imagined it would be this soon and under such sad circumstances. Though I was only given a few hours to prepare for this huge change, I feel completely honored and ready, as though I have been preparing my whole life for this day. I know that my decisions from now on will affect the lives of everyone in this room and that is why I have called this meeting.

"When I was a little girl, Daddy used to tell me about this very day, the day I would inherit it all and be to the family what he was. I was so proud, even back then, to know that one day I would be entrusted with all that we have. I used to tell him all the things I was going to do with the money and gold and land that we owned. I had big plans back then.

"Then I grew older and realized that he was only placing trust in me to take over one day because it was tradition, because it was what was done. Tradition — that word has haunted me for years. To me, it meant a pre-destined life, no choice, no say, no life at all. A practice that may have served well in prior days but surely didn't or wouldn't apply to me. And I was shocked when I realized that my one-day power wasn't because I was necessarily trustworthy and able to run the household but simply because I was born. And so my many dreams had been defeated and I gave up on the wonderful fantasies I had created as a child.

"For twenty years I lived a life that was created for me, knowing that when the time came, everything would continue to be taken care of for me, for us. I would marry whomever Daddy chose and life would continue as it always had; everything would be safe. But today, something ironic happened. I am here, unwed, and there is no man to make everything safe and done. It is just me and Daddy has said that that is good enough. I am trustworthy again. He has made the right decision. It is true; I own all of this but I don't own any of you. You are my family and I will not throw away your dreams for mine.

"The house will remain the same, with slight variations to the traditional rule, of course, and we will continue as we have for the last twenty years. I will review our assets and find room for investment in my own interests. From now on, extravagant parties will be fundraisers and my dreams will find a way into this world. Thank you all for your support. I love you so much and I want to do everything possible to keep us a family."

Chapter Twenty-six

"Shit Kay, I don't believe you." Johnny's grin was wide and confident. "You must've understood wrong, man. Madison isn't engaged. And she sure as hell isn't getting married. I know you don't like the idea of the two of us together, even if you are just covering your own ass. I completely understand where you're coming from. But this isn't about you or some stupid job, this is the girl of my dreams we're talking about here."

"Yeah, well, she ain't just appearing in your dreams, buddy. There are a million guys waiting for a chance at that one, and ones who don't sport grass stains and sweaty bandanas on a daily basis. You gotta face it, kid. A girl like that probably eats little shits like you for breakfast and then goes on to marry the billionaire next door. You hearing me?"

"Yeah, I hear ya. But you're wrong, Kay. For once, you're wrong. She's different. She doesn't fit into their mold like other spoiled rich kids. She isn't like that. And she's not getting married."

"Look, Johnny, maybe she is the sweetheart you say she is but the fact is, they'll marry the girl off a thousand times before they let her near the likes of you. And that's exactly what they've done. The old man's getting older and he's gotta protect what's his: his daughter and his fortune. We aren't part of that world, guys like us. We gotta work for bastards like them just to see tomorrow. It may be old money they're sitting on but it's money they have and we don't." Kay placed a hand on Johnny's stubborn shoulder. "You gotta look out for number one, kid. We've both been at the bottom of the food chain long enough to figure that one out. So, you let a little fun and fantasy distract you; you had a good time. You'll get over it and her and I'll see you back at work when this is all over and they're done trampling all the work we've done this season. Got it?"

"I'll see you, Kay, tomorrow morning, bright and early." Johnny waved Kay off with a look of annoyance in his eye. But as he continued to work, a worried crease began to form in his brow as he thought about Kay's words. Kay was an honest guy, Johnny knew, but he couldn't believe what the man was saying. He had to find Madison and let her reassure him that this was all just a misunderstanding.

Hadn't Madison told him of a close cousin once? It must be her wedding they were hosting in the garden. Man, Kay had really gotten the story wrong this time.

Johnny collected the rack and sacks he had been using to collect the colorful leaves autumn had been dropping. An annoying pulling in his stomach had him wrapping things up quick. Though he had convinced himself that it was all just some unfortunate mix-up, something in him, part fear, part anger, needed to find out what the hell was really going on. He had intended to give Madison the day to recover from her trip and enjoy the exotic paradise he had spent all night creating for her but this was too important. He had to see her. Now.

Al spotted Johnny and she had to admit, he was quite a sight. Filthy and glistening with sweat from a good morning's work, he marched straight for the mansion with nothing but determination on his face. She debated a moment then decided she had better head him off before he waltzed right into the Carlton kitchen and humiliated himself.

Johnny couldn't think. He knew he shouldn't be this close to the mansion in the middle of the day but he didn't care anymore. He was tired of skulking around in shadows, creeping about in silence, praying no one would see or hear him. He had to get Madison's attention somehow. They needed to talk.

"And where are you headed in such a hurry?" Al came up on Johnny's side and stepped right into beat with his long, quick strides.

"Beat it. I gotta take care of something, Al."

"Looks to me like you're headed straight for the snake pit. You know, it's too bad that girl took you for such a bad ride, honey, but you gotta admit it, this is best for everyone. You had your turn and you had your fun but the gig is up."

Johnny stopped dead in his tracks. "So Kay told you that bullshit story too? As soon as I get this sorted out I'm gonna kick that guy's ass to tomorrow."

"Hey, it isn't a story. It's the truth." Al pulled out her secret weapon then and handed it to him. "She's a lying bitch, Johnny, and she's been playing you all summer."

"What's this?" Johnny unfolded the thick

white card and read the glossy gold handwriting shining up at him.

Al had found the lot of them in a trash bin in the shed weeks ago. She figured they had been discarded when the wedding had been postponed after the old man went down with a stroke. And just when she thought she was going to have to devise a plan to separate Johnny and Madison for good, princess goes and takes care of everything, for all of them. Al had waited a long time for this moment and she was loving every second.

"What the hell is this?"

"An invitation, to your girlfriend's wedding, though I don't see your name on it anywhere."

"Where did you get this?" Growing more and more furious, Johnny demanded answers.

"It doesn't matter where it came from; it just is. Come walk with me, honey." Al draped an arm around Johnny's waist and gently steered him away from the mansion.

"But, I don't understand. This can't be right." Johnny stared at the fancy card, rereading the cheery words. He dragged a finger over Madison's name in disbelief, smearing it with dirt and sweat.

The date stood out and triggered memories of the early summer and of the time when Julian had fallen ill. Madison had been a wreck and he had seen her through it. Remembering his own father's sickness and eventual death, Johnny offered her the sympathy and strength that he himself had never known. He now wondered how many of her tears were shed for a postponed wedding.

"No, it's exactly right, for everyone. You go back to living your life, she can get on with her money and fame and Kay can quit worrying about how your little love affair will affect his next paycheck." She smiled then and gave his dirty shirt a little scratch. "And we can get back to how things used to be. You remember that, huh, when it was just you and me?"

Johnny was barely listening. His mind was racing, causing the confusion to grow until he doubted his entire relationship with Madison. He felt like a fool. They had all warned him and he hadn't listened. He had merely thought them jealous and ignorant. Yet now he held the proof of their hurtful words in the clutch of his fist and it burned like the hot anger that flowed through his every vein.

Johnny continued to fume as Al led him into his cabin and closed the door. She knew it would be impossible to get him to calm down right away so she sat herself comfortably on his unmade bed and let him pace. He was going to have a male tantrum. She had witnessed many and had been the cause of many more, but she wasn't going anywhere. For now, Al could sit back and enjoy the show. It had been too easy so far but her cue would soon come and she knew that when it did, she would need all the energy she could muster for a guy like Johnny.

"Fucking shit, Al! How could I be so stupid? It must have showed and that's how she did this to me. She knew I was stupid over her, from fucking day one. I can't believe I let the bitch know it too. She used me all summer, and I let her. Her damn entertainment after a boring day with the in-laws, a chance to let her hair down and step outta that stuffy suit. You know she didn't even wear makeup around me or goddamn underwear for that matter. Don't think daddy would have approved of that or her faggot fiancé. What was that asshole's name again?"

"Leemon, Arthur Leemon," Allison supplied.

"Aren't they the billionaires from three estates over? Leemon, huh? All fucking doctors and lawyers."

"Four centuries running." Al had done her homework.

"Man, Kay was right on with this one. Tried to tell me how it worked in these billionaire circles. She even told me herself, first time I met her. What was I thinking? She used me for a good time, attention, you know, the stuff she doesn't get back at the palace."

"Sounds pretty familiar to me."

"Yeah, yeah, go ahead with the I-told-you-sos. I deserve it after this one and don't try to keep Kay away either; he gets a round too." He dragged a defeated hand through his wild hair and Al's loins gave her a long, torturous pull. She loved it when a man looked as beaten as a scolded puppy and this was her cue.

"No, you don't. You didn't deserve any of this, Johnny. You're a great guy and that little slut's pretty dumb if she couldn't figure that one out. Thought she could pull tricks behind your back. Well she's going to find out you got a whole slew of friends watching out for you too."

"Yeah, I know it. Thanks." Finally calming down, Johnny looked into his friend's eyes, refusing the urge to look away when humiliation burned at the back of his throat.

"Well, I wasn't always there for you, so I thought I owed you one." Al lay back and let her massive head of curls rest on his pillow.

She knew he was going to get over this one. Too bad for her it was going to have to be on his time.

"We're even then," Johnny answered fairly and then let himself sit and fall back onto the bed beside Al.

"So, do you think she was ever going to tell you herself, or just let you find out when we get handed the garbage bags for cleanup?" she asked after a while and he really wondered as they both stared up at the ceiling above them.

"I don't know. Maybe she thought I was stupid enough to never find out and we'd go on meeting in the dead of night in her father's garden forever." He finally laughed at himself and the absurdity of the entire situation, a deep belly laugh that had him gulping for air and shaking the tiny bed beneath them. It was so contagious that Al couldn't help herself from rocking with giggles too. And when they finally stopped, exhausted and holding their aching sides, Al told him how proud she was of him in the only way she knew how.

"Hey, Johnny, you're doing pretty good. Haven't punched anything, broken much and you're not dripping. I think you just redeemed yourself. I was getting a little worried when that shark had her teeth in you."

"The day is still young, Allison," he said with serious eyes again. He hadn't cried yet, had done just about everything but that, but it was only a matter of time before the loneliness hit him.

"Oh no you don't," she proclaimed and jumped him. He was the ticklish type and she knew all the right spots. Laughing with him had felt so good that it erased all thoughts of Madison and what she had done to him. Al wasn't going to let her old friend feel sorry for himself when the best was yet to come.

With biceps that matched his own, Johnny had to fight to keep up with her. She was quick and knew just where to get him and he remembered the tickle fights they used to have in their own apartment years ago. Using his old strategy, as it came back to him, he finally managed to sit on both her knees and clasp her wrist up over her head. After maneuvering the trusty position, he simply held on for dear life until she became too exhausted to struggle anymore.

The late afternoon sunlight had filtered through the cabin's tiny window, warming everything in its path. Casting shadows and highlights over their glistening bodies. When Al finally huffed her signal for a fair surrender she looked dreamily up at him, watching the beads of sweat that had formed on his upper lip quiver. She was so thirsty and imagined lapping him up for hours in the stuffy room where they lay tangled in each other, hot and hungry.

"Is it always this hot in here?" she asked, her voice deep and husky from laughing it raw.

"Yeah, but mostly at sunset when the rays find me."

With her hair everywhere and her T-shirt hiked up and tangled in his, Johnny couldn't help himself. His eyes lingered over her lips where they were moist and full and seemed to whisper his name in every breath that passed through them. His gaze then shifted to her eyes that had clouded over until they were a seductive deep emerald hiding behind heavy lids and thick lashes. He breathed her in; she was all around him; her smell was everywhere. She was watching him watching her and, when his lips finally met hers, he felt the sweet pleasure of her muscles quiver beneath his own.

More memories flooded them both as his strong mouth moved farther in to devour hers. The transition from playful to passionate was so swift that neither of them had had time to think. They could only react to each other and that was exactly what they wanted. He needed her so badly that the large part of him begging him to stop hadn't stood a chance.

She needed to give him everything he wanted, everything he deserved, the instant his lips met hers. She let herself respond fully to every touch. Desperate hands slid over moist, hot skin, sending ripples of sensation throughout their greedy bodies, their excited loins.

Al could only close her eyes, throw her head back and let out a feline purr when Johnny caught her swelling breast in his hand and hungrily licked the aching point of her arousal with his hard, wet tongue.

"I want you so bad, Allison," he heaved and with one hard yank, had his jeans falling away from his trim waist.

"Then take me!" she demanded, daring him to take them both higher than they had ever gone before. She had already wiggled out of her own jeans by then and he noted that after all these years the girl still didn't own a pair of panties.

He plowed into her at her request and felt the first explosion of her pleasure go off.

"You gone soft on me, Red? Well, hold on cause there's more where that came from."

He was reckless and rough yet it only drove Al closer to the edge. She nipped his neck with her teeth and scraped her finger-nails down his muscled back, encouraging him to drive harder and faster. She was feeling a little reckless herself as she opened her eyes and saw Johnny enjoying the ride as well. Then and there, she decided it was time to celebrate.

Chapter Twenty-seven

Madison walked slowly yet proudly down the path to Johnny's cabin. It had been the longest two days of her life and it showed as she dragged her feet and fought to keep her head high. Her father wouldn't be buried until tomorrow and, after having taken care of all that was required of her, she needed to get away from the mansion.

Sunset fell on her as she walked the familiar stony path, graciously warming the chill in her bones, and she stopped briefly to lift her eyes and look around her. It was all hers, as far as she could see, and it was breathtaking. And that is how she planned to keep it. It would be one family tradition she would honor.

The grounds were so full of healing and history and beauty that she could imagine the sweet sound of laughter and joy in the air, lingering over years of Carlton ancestors. She pictured those who had come before her, strolling along the same paths and feasting on the same ripe and juicy fruits as she did today. Madison felt the magic of her heritage, its strength and prestige.

But the best part was walking in the glorious remains of the day, head high, to her love. She didn't have to hide any longer. Their love wasn't a secret among the family anymore and now, the staff would know and accept it too. And she couldn't wait to tell Johnny. She had so much to tell him, part good, part bad, but ultimately she had to tell him that she loved him and wanted to marry him. She wanted him to be part of her family, her world and she needed to be part of his.

They had finished early today, she noted, probably still under the orders of her mother and her mad attempt at throwing a surprise wedding. But that was all taken care of now. Elizabeth was still on the phone making the cancellation for the wedding and the preparations for the funeral. Her mother had been sedated by the doctor and out for the night. Madison would deal with her later.

Now, all she needed was to fall into Johnny's comforting arms and tell him all about it. She wanted him to stand beside her at the funeral, for her own support as well as for her family. He was going to be part of them now. It was going to take some getting used to but they had all the time in the world. She was in love, and among all the bad that had struck, her swelling heart seemed to make it all just bearable.

Madison came up on Johnny's door as the last of the day's sun was disappearing behind the tall pine trees that surrounded the estate. She gave the door a soft knock before hearing the muffled sounds that came from behind it. She panicked when she recognized the sound was Johnny and some kind of struggle. Lifting a fallen branch from the grass nearby, Madison wrapped her small hand around it, held it up over her head and threw open the cabin door.

"Oh —"

"Shit!" Johnny scrambled off Al and tried to pull the tangled bed sheet over his waist at the same time Al pulled on the cloth, trying to conceal her own exposed flesh.

"Madison? Is that you? Put that thing down, Jesus. Just calm down. It's not what you think —"

"That I can see. I thought you were being attacked, that you were hurt. I heard . . . But obviously you are feeling quite all right." Her voice broke then and she quickly turned and stepped out of the cabin. The evening had turned the air dark and cool but her body burned with anger and mortification and she didn't want to see anything clearly. She had seen enough.

As she darted away she heard him calling after her and she thanked the night for the darkness that shielded her from his face and for the coolness to soothe her raging head.

Johnny snatched the sheet from his bed, wrapped it around his middle and took off after her, leaving Al stumbling for her clothes in the darkness of the cabin.

"Madison, stop!" He wasn't too far behind her now and there was something in his voice that made her do just that. He wasn't pleading with her or apologizing; he was just as angry as she was.

"I don't believe you have anything to say that I would have an interest in listening to." She turned on him. He stopped a few feet from her and could barely make out her face, though he knew she was crying from the thickness in her voice.

"So, you think we have nothing to talk about, princess?" He almost spat the little pet name he called her. "Aren't you supposed to show off the rock? You know, be giddy and squeal and actually wear it?"

"What are you talking about?"

"The wedding ring, Madison. You're engaged and as good as married. The goddamn wedding is in a couple hours. Did you think I wouldn't find out? Do you think I'm that stupid? Well, I was, stupid enough to believe that we had something. What are you doing here anyways? Can't get any action from the old man?"

"How dare you!" she shouted and shoved at him so hard in the dark that he had to take a couple steps back to steady himself. He caught her wild wrists in his hands as he tried, blindly, to protect himself.

"Let go of me, you bastard." A quick kick to his shin had him releasing her and limping on one leg.

"Go ahead and run, still can't fess up to the truth!" he called out to her when she had walked away.

"You aren't worth that much," she called back into the blackness, not caring whether he had heard her or not.

"Rise and shine. Let's go, Johnny boy, I need you up and stationed in thirty minutes." Kay barged into Johnny's room as he had the rest of the crew's. They weren't in for a day off, after all, direct orders from a sweet, little old lady with silver hair and large rosy cheeks.

"Wow, what is that stink, Sparks?" Kay quickly spotted the empty liquor bottle.

Shaking his head, he pushed the little window farther open. His man was going to need fresh air and a long shower, even if he had to hose him down himself. And he did.

"Beat it, Kay. I quit." Still slurring his words and watching the room spin, Johnny could only growl fiercely when Kay picked him up by the scruff of his neck and dumped him under the icy spray of the shower.

"What's all this about?" Johnny was sobering up and sorry for it as the throbbing returned to his head and his shin. Memories of the night before were resurfacing and leaving a vile taste in his mouth. Al . . . and then Madison . . . Oh, and then that horrible bottle . . .

"Well it looks like our wedding just got swapped for a funeral. What I need you guys to do is man your stations by all the estate's incoming and outgoing streets. Cops are taking care of the screening but this one's going to be huge. Seems the old man finally kicked it. This ain't no private party anymore. We are going to need everyone —"

"Wait a minute. What did you just say? Julian Carlton is dead?" Johnny could only imagine Madison and what she was going through.

"Heard me right kid. So get changed and meet me —"

"The funeral's today? So that's gotta mean he's been dead a few days."

"Must have been, Sherlock. They probably didn't want the news to leak until they had the funeral arrangements set up. But anyways, like I was saying, we are going to need some hefty manpower. Media is welcome — they couldn't have kept them away — but only on the family's cue. Hey, you hearing me?"

"Yeah, yeah. We'll have everything under control."

"Just get yourself stationed in ten. I'm counting on you, buddy." Kay hurried off, though a little less than convinced that Johnny was going to have it all under control today.

Finally alone, Johnny dressed and tried to process what he had just heard. It was all a big puzzle and putting the pieces together was an awful feat when cheap liquor haunted your every movement.

That classy invite dated weeks ago, her early return, the old man's death. She had come to see him after her father had died and that's when she had found him and . . . He was more confused than ever. He needed answers and he knew just where to find them.

Chapter Twenty-eight

The somber music that played throughout the massive viewing was appropriately sad, although slightly hopeful and exactly how Madison had wanted it. It was a shame that her first call to power meant organizing a funeral for her own father but Elizabeth had been her rock through it all. She felt foolish now for looking to Johnny for comfort and understanding. She knew now that he couldn't have loved her. He was still in love with Al, a love that she had unmistakably witnessed firsthand and she wondered now how long that kind of love had been going on behind her back.

While the hordes of people came and went, paying their respects, Madison had time to think, so much time, in fact, that she was buckling up that belt and riding that emotional roller coaster for the hundredth time that day. She didn't know why she insisted on putting herself through so much anguish but the more she thought about it, the more things just didn't add up. If she and Johnny were through then why were there still so many unanswered questions?

Did he actually think she was getting married today, that she would go through with the arranged engagement to Arthur Leemon? And that she had planned to all the while, behind his back? And what about what she had found last night? He knew she was home early from her trip and would even be expecting her to pay him a visit to thank him for the flowers. Didn't he ever question why she was home so early?

So many lies. It reminded her that their entire relationship had been one big lie to her family. But she had cleared that up only to find that they had both been lying to each other as well. She about Arthur and he about Allison.

Madison looked around her. She had lost them both and it would be a long while before she was going to be okay with that. But she had duties and responsibilities now to get her through and without the pressure to marry Arthur — or anyone else — she also had her freedom and her own life to think about.

It was going to be okay, a fact she was surer of when she saw Elizabeth's flushed head poke out from the hall's kitchen and give her a sparkling wink.

"I'm very sorry for your loss, Ms. Carlton."

Madison automatically lifted her head and cheek to accept yet another condolence. Her mouth dropped when she met Johnny's sympathetic brown eyes.

"How did you get in here?" she asked coldly after recovering from the shock and accepting his kiss, so as not to make a scene.

"I know a few secret entrances." He was holding up the line and her hand a little too tightly. All eyes were now on Madison and the new stranger. She quickly took his arm and steered him out of the hall and into a doorway, away from the crowd.

Joseph had seen the unfamiliar face and Elizabeth had to step in his path to stop him from intervening.

"All is well, my dear. He is certainly welcome here." She patted the lapels of his dark suit and waited for the understanding to relax his tense muscles.

"Is there something I could help you with, Mr. Sparks?" Madison asked him coolly.

"Elizabeth told me everything. I know about the arranged marriage and your mother and now your father. I really am sorry. By what you've told me, he must have been a hero."

"That still doesn't change the fact that you lied about Al," she responded icily.

"And you lied about being engaged. Look, I never lied about Al. We had something, me and her, but that was years ago. That's over now, I promise. I love you. Did you know that?"

"I thought I did. I even thought I might have loved you back. Must have been a bad piece of chicken, but I'm over that now."

"Don't do this, princess."

"I will do whatever I want, whenever I want. It's my party, remember?"

"Yeah, I remember. I remember a very wise man saying that exact thing to the love of his life."

"Don't say that . . . don't you realize how much it hurt me when I found you and . . ."

"Ah huh! So you do love me."

"Of course I love you. I was coming by last night to tell you just that, but —"

"No buts. It was a mistake, a big one. I was messed up over the wedding invitation and then Kay . . . Anyways, I'm sorry. Really sorry."

"Wedding invitation?"

"Yeah, Al got a hold of one somehow and Kay was still on your mother's orders and I thought you were really going to marry that loser —"

"Al and Kay?" Madison shook her head in confusion.

"They were just trying to look out for me. Had this theory about you and your family. Seems they were right on with your mother. I'm glad they were wrong about you though. I'll forgive you if you forgive me."

"I don't know if I can. I just don't know if I can forget . . . I want to, so badly."

"You don't have to. Forgive but never forget and I promise I will spend the rest of my life making it up to you."

He bridged the gap between them and kissed her lightly on her forehead. "You are everything to me."

"Could we start over?"

"I think we should," he agreed.

"And this time it won't be a secret anymore —"

"You mean —"

"Yup, I told them all."

"And?"

"I think they are getting used to the idea."

"Good." He looked around the massive hall, from the marble floors to the antiques and endless walls of paintings and then back to her smiling face. "So am I."